DARK FAE UNRIVALED

BROKEN COURT BOOK THREE

HEATHER RENEE

CONTENTS

DEDICATION

For Jamie Holmes.
My bestie.
My person.
My editor.
My hotel buddy.
I love you to the moon and back!

CHAPTER 1

Serving assholes the punishment they deserved used to bring me a joy I couldn't find anywhere else. It had come naturally to me after being banished from the fae realm. More importantly, it had been simple—black and white. For so long, all that had mattered was doing what was right, even if it wasn't good.

Sometime during the last month or so, I'd lost that elation, and there were trickles of grey filtering into my mind. Especially now that I was certain I should have been dead but wasn't. I did my best to sort out my emotions after coming back from the castle on my own, but I'd had enough solitary time after spending most of it healing myself without extra help. I'd refused to let Olida touch me again.

When Ivy woke up and told me I'd done exactly what Zephyr had hoped I'd do, I wanted to scream and burn everything to the ground. It had never been my intention to do anything for the benefit of the king, but the darkness I'd let in—or maybe it was out—had saved my life as well as Ivy's. I was trying not to be pissed the hell off or take out my rage on anyone else, which was why I'd stayed alone for the last couple days. Or so I thought. Time hadn't really been relevant.

As soon as we had arrived back at Mosi's island with a very-much-alive Ivy, I went straight for the trees, keeping the sword with me because the thought of parting with it made me physically ill. I knew I should have been concerned with that but hadn't wanted to focus on it yet.

Hours passed as I stared between the branches, waiting. For what exactly, I wasn't quite sure. I knew I at least had to be back in control of my actions, though. When the sun began to rise for the second time since our return, I'd finally felt like myself again.

Though, who I was… I wasn't even sure if I knew at that point.

While I'd enjoyed my seclusion, I was surprised Finn had never come for me. My heart physically hurt for him—the bond punishing me for staying away—and I wasn't sure what to think about that. Several times, he'd walk through the forest, but not once had he stopped or called for me. I didn't understand it, and a part of me felt betrayed, as if being away from me hadn't affected him whatsoever.

Even if the bond was causing me pain, at least it hadn't stopped me from healing the rest of the physical wounds I'd received back at the castle in the fight against Gabriel.

Ha! You wish. You only have me to thank for you still breathing, my inner voice cut in.

Gods, how had I missed that annoyance at any point?

Even if the voice was right, I would give some credit to the sword strapped to my hip. It had brought me back to life, or at least I thought it had. That was something I hadn't been able to sort out while I was staying amongst the trees.

Why hadn't I died? Gabriel had delivered a fatal wound at the same time I struck a dagger into his skull. I should have been killed along with him, but there I was. Walking, breathing, and still me.

It was time for answers that I knew I could only get from Mosi and Olida. The hair on my neck stood just thinking about Olida. I'd liked her—like, really liked her. And when Neva had said my inner voice had been suppressed, not stripped away by the bond, I was furious. Yet, I knew I'd changed, and I was trying to be calm enough to figure things out before causing the destruction I wanted to. If Olida truly had lied to me and done more than she'd let on, she was going to have to answer for her deception.

My wings unfurled as my boots crunched over the fallen leaves on the dirt ground of the forest. I stomped more than necessary, but I kept my anger in check.

The darkness within me had been urging me to kill all who tried to change me, including Finn. It was more intense than ever before and not something I had anticipated, but I'd figured out how to block out the worst of it. Being in control was most important to me as I moved forward.

I was prepared to ask questions first before reacting. Something I wouldn't have done a month ago. While I'd been adamant that I loved who I was before and didn't want to change, I'd come to realize that was just me living in fear. Fear of the unknown and allowing anyone the power to hurt me.

The closer I got to the island huts, the higher the anticipation. The bond that tied me to Finn grew deeper by the day, and I'd nearly lost control of my own actions earlier in the day when I'd sensed him nearby. Even as I moved through the trees, my wings began to move of their own accord, and I found myself flying to where I assumed everyone to be.

My heart pounded in my chest, my emotions twisting together, and I thought I was going to have another panic attack, but as soon as I crashed into a hard body, I was back in warrior mode. Well, until I realized who I'd flown into.

"Lucy? Are you okay?" Finn asked, his hands roaming over my arms and up to my face as I stared into his silver eyes. "I was just headed—"

I didn't let him finish. The need of the bond was uncontrollable after days without touching my other half. I tucked my wings away, jumped and wrapped my legs around him before delivering a bruising kiss he hadn't been expecting. Not that he seemed to have any problem returning it.

One of Finn's arms wrapped around my ass, and the other settled over my shoulder blades, holding me impossibly close as a warmth filled my body that only Finn could elicit.

Gods, I'd missed him. I'd never thought that was possible. Even if it might have been the bond controlling my actions, I knew Finn was a good person, one who cared for me in a way no one before him had. While I didn't understand why he hadn't come for me, it didn't lessen what I knew existed between us. What I had spent hours thinking about while hanging out in the trees.

"I missed you," he murmured against my cheek before he kissed his way down my neck.

I grabbed a fistful of his hair, yanking his head back with one hand and digging my nails into his shoulder with the other. "Then, why didn't you come for me?"

He floundered for a moment. "I did. I searched for you, but I couldn't find you anywhere on the island."

The inner voice chuckled in my mind.

What did you do? I snapped.

He could have tried harder if he really cared and you know it, the voice responded.

"Lucinda?" Finn asked, wincing as my grip tightened.

I loosened my hold, letting my body slide down his. "It doesn't matter now. It's time to find out what Mosi and Olida have really been up to."

Finn didn't release me. "I know you're upset. Neva told us what she thought Olida did, but I promise, that's not the case."

While I might have been enjoying being in Finn's arms, this was something I couldn't take his word for. "We'll see about that."

I leaned up and distracted him with another kiss before teleporting myself to the huts. It was what I should have done to begin with, though I wouldn't deny that having Finn be the first person I saw wasn't a bad thing.

When I arrived at the huts, I heard laughter coming from Mosi and Olida's house.

They're laughing at you. End them, the voice broke through my thoughts.

Go away, I snarled back.

Okay, maybe my control wasn't as solid as I wanted, but it didn't matter. I was done hiding, done waiting for answers.

The voice's snickering faded away as I managed to push it further from my mind. I had to deal with Olida first.

I burst through the door with Finn right behind me. I'd known he would follow and was glad he hadn't tried to stop me. Instead, he stood by my side as I eyed the room before me.

Neva, Ivy, Maddox, Olida, and Mosi sat on pillows with an array of food between them and steaming cups of something that smelled divine.

Mosi saw me first, and he wrapped an arm around Olida. "Lucinda, it's nice to have you back."

Olida raised her chin, and Neva scrambled to her feet. She was wearing a white linen outfit like the other fae here often did and seemed to be fitting right in. "It's okay, Lucy. Calm down." Her hands reached for me, but she winced as they made contact. "Lucy?"

I could hear the fear in her voice, but my eyes wouldn't stray from Olida. I was furious with the fae who peered back at me like I was a monster. She'd tried to kill me. She'd taken away my voice. I wouldn't let her do so again.

The sword at my side warmed as sparks of magic responded to my rage. I took a step forward, but Neva's outburst gave me pause.

You will never control me, the voice whispered, but before I could figure out why, chaos ensued.

"Now, Finn!" Neva shouted, backing away from me.

I turned around just in time to see the dagger in Finn's hand as he sliced through the belt I'd made from vines for the sword. The long silver blade clattered to the ground, and he kicked it out the door, Neva following after it.

As I tried to do the same, I fell to my knees, pain rocking through me just like when we'd been in the castle. My hands gripped my head and pressed tightly, as if I could make it go away. Every ounce of fury was replaced by agony.

Quit fighting me and this wouldn't hurt as bad, the voice sneered as I shook my head.

Warmth from Finn's body pressed against my back as his arms wrapped around me. "It's okay, Lucinda. I'm here and you're safe."

As the pain lessened from his touch, so did the rage that had taken over when I stormed through the door.

Well, most of it. No, only some of it.

"What the hell is happening to me?" I roared as I struggled to choose between embracing the calmness Finn provided and the need to kill everything in my path.

No one responded as they watched me with wary eyes.

The darkness must have given me a false sense of control back in the trees. It would have known what I wanted, and I'd let it trick me.

The tighter Finn held me against his chest, the more I was finally able to see reason, but it wasn't without effort. A fog I hadn't known was there lifted from my mind, making me a little more rational while still being frustrated as hell. My fists shook as things began to make more sense about my inner voice.

Neva crept back into the hut, staying as far from me as she could, and set the sword on the counter. I flinched to grab it, but Finn didn't release me, even after I elbowed him. Twice.

As I considered fighting my way toward the only thing that part of me believed brought me true peace, Mosi inched closer with Olida behind him. "It's okay, Lucinda. We didn't know before, but we do now."

"Know what?" I growled, forgetting about the

sword and remembering how much I wanted to hurt them for deceiving me.

That's right, Lucinda. Remember how they wronged you.

I snarled in frustration as Neva reached for me again, but she didn't back down, this time having no problem touching me as her hand rested on my arm for a moment. "Come sit with us."

She and Finn urged me from the entryway floor as Mosi and Olida backed off again. Ivy and Maddox were staring at me as we walked closer, but there was no judgement in their faces, only empathy.

Maddox nodded at me, his green eyes softening. "I'm sorry I tried to kill you."

I took a deep breath, fighting the need to rip his face off, and managed to shrug. "I would have done the same."

Finn huffed as he held on tighter to me, the bond flaring to life again as his cheek pressed against my exposed shoulder. I focused on him, building a mental wall between the worst of the darkness and the last of my sanity.

When I felt more in control, or so I hoped, I allowed Finn to pull me into the living room. There was only one pillow left that he sat down on first while tugging me onto his lap. Even though I'd thought a lot about the bond while I'd been alone and was certain I was ready to embrace it the best I could, I still wasn't a fan of this kind of public affection.

I tried to move to the floor, but his hold increased. "I

don't think so." His voice was rough and commanding, sending a wave of desire through me.

Nobody said anything about our position, so I let it slide and focused back on Mosi and Olida. "It's time for you to spill what you know, Mosi. Screw whatever rules you have about the future. You better tell me what the two of you did to me, why I'm all of a sudden hurting without that damn sword or Finn, and how the hell I brought Ivy back to life. If you don't, I'm going to fight a lot harder to get my hands on that sword again."

I knew Mosi held information I needed to understand what was happening to me and killing his mate wouldn't get me what I wanted. Though, I hadn't expected that just seeing her would enrage me like it had.

I hadn't thought the inner me had so much control over my actions, either.

As usual, nothing was as it seemed, which put me even more on edge.

Mosi nodded. "We will get to all of that, but we're going to start with my mate first, so I don't have to worry about you cutting her head off when I'm not looking."

He grimaced, and I smirked. "Well, maybe she shouldn't do things to people while they're unconscious that she has no business doing and nobody would be trying to cut her."

"Lucy, I would never intentionally harm you," Olida said, holding my stare without cowering away from the glare I sent her way like most supernaturals would have.

"Then what the hell did you do to me?" I barked and threw my hands out, almost smacking Neva in the face. "I was perfectly fine before I woke up on this island."

Before I did something else with my hands—like murder someone with stray magic—I grabbed bread from the tray in front of me and side-eyed what I assumed to be a mug of hot toddy based on the smell of spices wafting toward me. As the fluffy bite of bread melted into my mouth, I waited, not so patiently, for Olida to explain herself. She had until the slice was gone to convince me not to do just as Mosi feared.

You're weak and pathetic for allowing this, the voice strained, breaking through my block.

Gods, maybe I was going to murder myself instead just to shut the damn thing up.

"I healed you and calmed the rage within you, but I didn't know about the other side of you when you were bleeding to death on my floor. I only did what I had to in order to make sure you didn't die," Olida said, but I could see a hesitation in her eyes.

"And?" I asked.

She sighed. "Don't throw a fit," she warned first, and I chuckled.

"Go on." I waved a hand at her, taking another bite, half of the bread gone now.

"Well, now that I know more about you and what's going on, I think what I did might have possibly made you more susceptible to accepting the bond with Finn by inadvertently silencing the darker part of you. Never once did I mean for anything I did to further cause you harm, though."

My face lost all emotion as I thought about how her statement made me feel. I'd remembered there being a moment of clarity before the bond fully formed, when I knew I could have stopped things but chose not to. Had that been my true choice? Did it really matter if it wasn't?

During my hours in the jungle, I wasn't oblivious to the fact I was supposed to be dead. I'd been given a second chance and, while I still wanted to be me, I was firmly against continuing to live in fear. I'd been doing that for far too long.

I wanted to be with Finn, and that came with risks I needed to accept as well. But my bond with Finn wasn't why I was sitting in that hut. Olida's actions were. Everyone else seemed to believe she hadn't meant to make things worse, and I held her stare trying to decide if I could as well. With the inner voice pushed down, I thought I had enough clarity to decide on my own, but given how I'd lost it when I walked in their house, I wasn't sure how much I could believe.

Her lavender eyes sparked with mischief still, but it wasn't of the malicious sort. It never had been. She'd only ever tried to give me advice and accepted when I still wanted to do things my way. Olida was another risk I was letting into my life if I chose to let things go.

After dying, or whatever happened to me, I'd made

a choice to stop fighting the things in life that could bring me joy. I had to accept that I couldn't always keep my feelings safe from the kind of hurt I'd experienced after Zephyr had tossed me out like the previous day's trash.

I'd only been so raging about Olida's supposed betrayal because I cared for her. That was something I wasn't used to and didn't always know how to handle correctly, but I was trying—once again—not to live in fear.

Neva, the one I'd relied on and cared for the longest, continued to stare at me as I considered the options before me: continue to be afraid of the unknown or trust those around me. She nodded at me with those honey eyes that had always seen more of me than I liked.

She believed she had been wrong about Olida's actions. She trusted these people. It was time I tried harder to as well.

Finn's fingers dug into my thighs, as if he was nervous about how I'd react to Olida's news, but it wasn't necessary.

"It's whatever now. We can't change the past, but we can do something about the future. So, what other secrets are the two of you keeping?" I asked, keeping my voice even and calm. I might have been okay with Olida's healing mishap, but I wasn't stupid enough to believe they didn't have other secrets that affected me.

Olida stared me down with her familiar smirk, seeming to see more than she had the right to. I had a killer poker face, and I wouldn't be divulging anything I didn't want to until I was good and ready.

Mosi cleared his throat, getting my attention. "We believe you're in pain because of the dark magic. The castle is being shielded with a heavy power that isn't natural to any kind of fae I've ever known. It's a spell made from several forms of magic, and you began to have a reaction to it from what we were told. Then, being closer to the sword changed things for you, yes?"

"It did and clearly having it taken away outside of the castle didn't put me back to normal. I'm assuming you know why," I stated, casting a quick glance at the sword across the room. My fingers still itched to reach for it, but Finn's hold on me was stronger.

The door slammed open. "They think they know why, but only I do."

CHAPTER 2

*Y*ury stood over all of us with arms crossed, his head nearly touching the ceiling. He was still rocking the socks with sandals. "You couldn't even let your toes free while enjoying the island life?" I asked blandly.

"Jungle is dirty," he huffed, the Russian accent coming out strong.

Craning my neck up to have a conversation with him wasn't going to work for me, so I moved to stand, and Finn followed, never letting go of me. "So, Not Witch. What do you know?"

He glared at the sword Neva had left on the counter. "That weapon is evil and needs to be destroyed."

No!

The singular words echoed through my mind, but I couldn't tell if it came from me or the inner voice as I lunged toward the sword without thinking twice.

Finn jerked me back. "Not a good idea, Lucinda."

"I won't let him destroy it," I snarled, the darkness within me swelling and breaking through my walls until my entire body vibrated with the drive to get free.

Get the sword and kill them all, the voice snarled, then calmed and continued in a soothing voice, *Don't forget what's important, Lucinda.*

Whatever was inside me was almost too good at enticing me and making me want to listen. Almost, but not quite. I was stubborn enough to push it back down and think for myself, even if my actions didn't always follow immediately.

"She is worse than I thought. We must remove the dark magic from her," Yury said, taking a step toward me.

I raised my palm and lashed out at him with my own power. "Like hell you are. I've had enough people mess with me. There won't be any others."

"Little fae, you do not understand. I don't need to do this. Hell, I shouldn't do this, but Mosi has convinced me it is the only way. If I am to stay, you need to be stripped of the magic that does not belong to you," Yury said, not at all deterred by my little outburst.

"What do you mean doesn't belong to me?" I asked as Finn's grip on my arms increased and my indigo hair fell in front of my face.

"Mosi told me you are neither light nor dark fae, but you are drowning in a darkness that didn't exist when I first met you like it does now. The sword and the castle have tainted your very being, causing whatever was already there to grow significantly in power. Unless you want to constantly be at war with yourself and your decisions, then you need to have the magic removed," Yury answered.

I stood a little taller, my chest heavy from exertion. "I'm not at war with myself. I'm very much in control."

Yury scoffed. "Yeah, like Bruce Banner is in control. You are angry like Hulk."

That actually made me smile.

"Alright, Not Witch. So what if I am? I've been angry for a hell of a long time. How do you think you can fix me?" I asked.

"I need your blood and the sword to know for sure, but the same spell I need to use on Ivy should work on you, too, *Hulk,*" he replied, straight-faced even when using what seemed to be a new nickname for me.

I glanced back at Ivy and Maddox. "You're still dealing with that shit? I wondered if whatever I did to bring you back might have made the sickness go away as well."

"That would have been nice, but apparently, you're not that cool." Ivy winked at me.

I shrugged. "I'm perfectly okay with that."

"Your power is not that of a regular healer, Lucinda," Mosi said. "In fact, you're not a healer at all, just like I'm not a seer. We have versions of these abilities that defy any regular understanding of them, but what I've learned makes more sense after what's happened."

"And what would that be?" I asked.

"You can only bring back those who are not meant to die. I've seen visions of the fight against Zephyr, and we are all present. Of course, what I see doesn't always come to fruition, but it is rare. If Maddox, Finn, or Ivy would have died before the fight, it would have changed things drastically. It wasn't their time yet, and you corrected what should have never happened."

"So, I'm not a necromancer or a healer. I'm just a twisted version of both?" I laughed, because I'd met a necromancer once before and that was the only supernatural to ever freak me the hell out. Of course, I would be similar to one of them. Karma was a bitch like that.

Mosi fought a grin. "You can look at it that way, but it's not like you go digging up bodies to bring people back. Their souls still have to be present."

"Well, she did dig up one body," Maddox joked, then sobered. "I remember when I was under the dirt, I thought I was going crazy because I was stuck in a nothingness. I guess my soul knew better than to move on before help arrived."

Ivy squeezed his hand, and they made googly eyes at each other just as I brought my attention back to Yury. "So, if you strip me of this darkness, will that change my abilities?"

"I do not know," he answered, and I appreciated his honesty.

"So, let me get this all straight. I don't have to kill Olida for screwing with me, Ivy could still die at any minute, I'm filled with a dark magic that doesn't belong to me, and we still need to kill Zephyr. Does that sound about right?" I asked, because there were too many people in this little hut tossing out information for my liking.

Olida stepped forward—much to Mosi's dismay—and gripped my chin, and I stared down at her smaller frame. No words were spoken. She just smiled at me, wrinkles forming around her light eyes, and her perfect teeth standing out against her darker skin.

"Olida, love. I think that's enough," Mosi said, inching closer to us.

She shooed him away with her other hand. "Me and Lucinda are having a moment." Then, she winked at me and I nodded.

A part of me—likely the bits I didn't have control over—still didn't want to trust her, but as she held my attention with her love and wisdom, I couldn't find it in me to listen to that part. Not even my inner voice could convince me she was a bad seed.

Olida never meant me any harm. I knew that deep in my soul. Just because I was afraid to believe didn't make it less true.

"I'm glad I don't have to kill you," I said, reaching to squeeze her elbow.

She released my chin and patted my cheek. "I'm sure glad you don't have to try anyway. Now, are you going to let us get that crap out of you, or are you going to make us wait for it to become your idea?"

A heaviness pulsed in my head, causing me to sway as I reached for Ivy when she tried to sneak past me with Maddox. "No. Ivy needs to be healed first. It's why Neva found Yury to begin with." As I said the words, the pressure eased.

Ivy glanced back at me, a frown on her face and a sadness in her eyes I hadn't noticed when I first walked in. "I am not the one who will save us. You first, then me. I won't let it be any other way." Then, she jerked her wrist from my hold and disappeared out the door with Maddox right behind her.

"What the hell was all that about?" I asked.

Neva stepped forward this time. "Ivy went through things I'm sure only you can understand. She's been resistant to opening up, but it hasn't been long, so we're not pushing. She is also worried Yury won't be able to strip the poison from her *and* the darkness from you no matter how hard we try to convince her otherwise," Neva said, and Yury grunted in response.

I was fully aware of what went on within the castle walls when Zephyr wanted to punish someone, but even with my understanding, I still thought she was being an idiot. The longer the poison was in her, the higher chance she had of dying at any moment.

Pounding began in my head, and I wavered again even though Finn hadn't removed his hold on me.

You are not strong enough to fight me. I will get what I want. We will kill the king and take his place, the voice demanded.

Yes, we will kill the king, I replied, and the throbbing eased while I hoped my internal battle had gone unnoticed.

That was the first time it had mentioned taking Zephyr's place. I had no desire to rule the fae. I didn't want that power or responsibility. If that's what the darkness within me was after, it was going to be sorely disappointed.

Only time will tell, it added.

When I was able to focus back on the others around me, Yury was glaring at me, keeping a distance while Neva stayed as close as possible.

Olida stepped closer to me, handing me a cup. "Drink this."

I eyed the steaming tea. "What's in it?"

"Something to make you feel more like yourself until you figure out what you want to do. You need to make the decision to strip the darkness on your own," she replied.

My hand twitched to knock the cup away.

Don't do it!

Piss off, I replied, then chugged the drink without thinking twice.

Screams sounded in my head but faded as the hot liquid moved down my throat and through my chest before settling at my core. *Ahh*, that was much better.

Olida nodded as Finn tugged me closer. If anyone else knew what was happening, they did a damn fine job pretending otherwise.

"We do this now," Yury demanded.

I wagged a finger at him. "I don't think so, Not Witch. My body, my choice." I was already going to say yes. I wanted my thoughts to be my own again, but still, there were people in this room I trusted, and I wanted their opinion.

"What do you think?" I asked Neva. She'd known me the longest out of anyone around, and I wanted the unbiased opinion I knew she'd give.

"I think it's a risk. Yury isn't sure of the ramifications to removing the darkness. If he does this and it takes too much of your power, we will be at a disadvantage when it comes to going after Zephyr again. But, if everything goes right, you could regain full control over your actions, and it just might be what we need to win," Neva answered methodically.

I glanced at Mosi. Even though I didn't entirely trust him, I wanted to hear his thoughts. "Can you see the right decision?"

He shook his head. "Like I said, I am not all-seeing. This is something you'll have to choose for yourself."

Turning toward Finn, I didn't even have to question him before he spoke. "You know the right thing to do here. Don't ask me, because I won't give you my opinion. As Mosi said, this is your choice to make."

Well, that wasn't as helpful as I'd hoped it would be, but maybe the choice was just that simple. Not everything right had to be hard.

"Okay, then. Yury, how do we do this?" I asked as a wave of nausea rolled through my stomach. Instead of hearing his answer, I lurched forward, throwing up whatever tea Olida had just given me all over her floor.

Finn moved to adjust his hold, but it was too late. Without the extra help to keep the darkness at bay, I lost control. Within a split second, my actions and thoughts were once again no longer my own.

I jerked out of Finn's hold and shoved Neva across the room as I turned around. My eyes landed on the sword, and a glee filled me as I lunged for it.

Power slammed into my side just as my fingertips touched the hilt, knocking me just out of reach from what I wanted most—no, what the darkness inside me wanted most. As the seconds ticked by, I was having a hard time differentiating between the two.

Pain from not only the blast but being separated from both Finn and the sword was growing. I took a step forward to find Finn and Yury moved in front of me.

My lips curled into a snarl. "Get out of my way."

"Not a chance in hell, Lucy. Fight this. Don't let the darkness be stronger than you are," Finn said.

I tossed my head and screamed as loud as possible. Sparks of magic radiated off me as my breathing increased and I fought through the agony and for power over my own body.

"You can't control me," I said aloud, but I was unsure of who I was actually speaking to.

"I already do." My voice projected, but it wasn't my own anymore—it was the darkness.

Magic filled me, lifting my feet up off the ground as my wings extended, knocking frames off the walls in the small space. I searched for the sword once again, but it wasn't on the counter where I last saw it. I searched for its power and moved forward, sensing it near.

Finn tried to stop me, his hands out and magic mingling with mine, but I merely laughed in his face.

"Oh, honey. You might be good in bed, but that's about it. Now get the hell out of my way," I taunted, snapping my fingers and enjoying the sight of Finn's body crashing through the open door.

Mosi, Olida, and Neva had scampered off at some point, so it was just me and the Russian left. I needed him dealt with so I could find the damn sword and be on my way.

I stepped closer to him, keeping my magic contained, hoping to use him. "Yury, darling. You're more powerful than these people deserve. Why don't you come with me and we can take the castle for ourselves?" I ran a finger down his chest, licking my lips.

He smiled, the first one I'd ever seen him offer, and it didn't help his appearance, but when his palms cradled my cheeks, I knew I had him.

"I thought you were smarter than that, Hulk," Yury said, then twisted his hands until my neck cracked, and everything went dark.

CHAPTER 3

When I came to, I didn't remember what had happened immediately. It wasn't until I figured out that my eyes were covered, my mouth was gagged, and the rest of me was strapped to what I assumed was a wooden table that everything came flooding back.

"Hulk is awake," Yury's voice mumbled as I jerked on the restraints. "And I don't think she is happy."

See? They don't trust you. Look at what they've done to us, my inner voice hissed.

Fuck. You.

I'd lost control once more, and that pissed me the hell off. Never once had I believed the darkness was stronger than me, but I'd been fooled. I wouldn't let it happen again.

"Lucinda, you in there?" Olida asked.

My head was also tied down, so I wasn't sure how she expected me to answer her.

Cool fingers settled in my hand. "Squeeze once for yes and twice for no."

"How are you going to know it's really her?" Neva's voice sounded as I squeezed twice.

I could hear the smile in Olida's voice. "Because she said no."

The blindfold came off first, and then the gag. "That's all you get until we know it's safe. You destroyed my house." Olida glared down at me, but there was more concern than anger in her soft eyes.

"Yeah, well, that's what you get for inviting a psycho like me in. Where's Finn?" I asked, remembering how I'd blasted him out the door. I didn't think I could have really hurt him, but seeing as he wasn't around, doubts filtered in.

"He's fine. He and Mosi went to get some items for Yury from the jungle. They should be back any minute," Neva answered, moving into view.

He left you. She's lying, the voice taunted.

I bit the side of my cheek, ignoring the doubts as Neva's honey eyes met mine. Her ebony curls shielded her face from everyone but me as I took in just how worried she'd been.

"I'm fine, Neva. I promise," I said.

"Yes, you will be. Just as soon as Yury is done with you," she replied with a slight smile before backing up.

"How am I not dead? Did I heal myself again?" I asked, knowing Yury had snapped my neck in order to gain the upper hand earlier.

Like you could do anything without me.

The inner voice was irate, but I did my best to ignore it, hoping that was the right choice.

Yury chuckled darkly from across the room. "I paralyzed you. You did not die."

I glared at him. "You shouldn't laugh or smile. It's not pretty on you, Not Witch."

He moved closer so I could see him, then grinned widely. The movement made his scars more prominent and his unibrow raised halfway up his forehead. "I have never tried to be pretty."

Bastard was seriously creepy.

Finn and Mosi arrived then, and Finn came straight to me after tossing Yury a bag. "You're awake." He sighed.

"Yeah, and hopefully I can walk after this, considering the oaf over there said he paralyzed me," I grumbled, trying to figure out if I could actually feel my legs, or if it was just a memory playing tricks on reality.

"I'll kill him myself if you can't." Finn grinned.

"Did I hurt you before?" I asked when I noticed dried blood on the collar of his white t-shirt.

"Nothing that didn't heal on its own," he replied.

My stomach rumbled, and my mouth was dry. "How long was I out?"

Olida appeared, cup in hand. "Just the afternoon. Night fell only an hour ago, but we were afraid to give you anything to drink if you were still paralyzed. You might have drowned or choked, and we'd have been none the wiser until you stopped breathing."

Well, that was fun news.

Olida nudged a straw to my lips, and when I didn't immediately open, she forced it in. I smelled the whiskey and took greedy gulps of her spiked tea, enjoying the gleam in her eyes. It was hard to swallow while laying down, but I managed to take several pulls without choking before she took it away.

"We'll feed you as soon as Yury is done," Olida said, backing out of my sight.

You won't make it to your next meal. You can't kill me without killing yourself.

Gods, the voice was getting harder to ignore, but I refused to give it any more power as I glanced back at Finn. "Why didn't you guys strip the darkness from me while I was unconscious? Wouldn't that have been easier?"

"Neva and I wouldn't let them without your permission again. It didn't feel right," Finn answered, brushing a stray hair from my cheek.

Yury grunted and muttered, "Pains in the ass."

"My pain in the ass," I whispered and enjoyed the charcoal that bled into Finn's eyes as the words registered with him. Before he could respond, though, Yury pushed him out of the way.

"Time to kill the fae. Stay back."

I told you so, the voice snickered.

Fucking hell, I thought more to myself.

Mosi grabbed Finn as he roared, "What did you say?"

"Do not worry. She should come back," Yury answered as even I began to panic a little.

"It's okay, Finn, I…" Neva's voice trailed off as they got further away from me.

Olida appeared at my head again and cupped her hands around my face. "The alcohol should help calm your nerves."

"You're evil," I sneered, but there was no hatred behind my words. Even with Yury's shitty bedside manner and the voice trying to convince me otherwise, I didn't believe they'd let me die if it was possible. They needed me to kill Zephyr. At least, I assumed they still did.

"I thought that's what you liked most about me." She winked and, before I could form a reply, Yury stabbed me in the damn stomach.

Believe me now, bitch?

And my inner voice had resorted to name-calling. Just great.

My body jerked, but I was still tied down as anguish erupted from me. "What the hell, Olida? I'm going to kill you!" I screamed, completely myself. "Finn! Neva!"

Olida at least had the audacity to look ashamed, but she didn't loosen her hold on my face. Her hands warmed as my arms shook, trying but failing to get free of the restraints. When that didn't work, I continued to shout.

Yury tsked. "They cannot hear you, but yell all you want. It will tire you out faster for me."

Olida turned back toward Yury and glared at him like a mother would at a disobedient child. "Hurry up just in case you're wrong," she hissed at him while still holding on to me.

"I am never wrong," Yury replied as he yanked the bloodied blade from my gut and set it just out of reach from my fingertips.

"I'm going to kill you both when I heal from this," I growled.

That's right, Lucinda. Focus on the rage, and we'll be out of here in no time, the inner voice encouraged.

Olida's hands began to burn my skin. "Yury, she's too strong. You need to hurry."

There was a tugging sensation on my stomach, and then I screamed, black magic shooting out of my mouth and smacking Olida in the face. Her hold broke, and power surged into me.

I had to get free. I could only trust myself. These people needed to die for hurting me.

One by one, the straps holding me down broke. Even though I was bleeding from my stomach, I paid the wound no attention, shoving Olida out of my way as I jumped off the table.

You can handle this. We'll heal later. I'll take care of you, the voice cooed.

Just me and my darkness. That was all I needed.

Yury charged toward me, his big frame casting a shadow over me, but he wasn't intimidating. I unfurled my wings and thrust my arms out. Instead of my normal magic, inky fog came out, stronger than anything I'd ever wielded.

"Well, Yury. Thanks for giving me an upgrade. Sorry,

I have to kill you now." I slammed my hand into his chest when he reached for me.

"You can try." He groaned beneath the pressure of my power.

Next, I placed both of my hands on his head, seeping black magic into him until he fell to his knees. Insignificant traces of doubt began to surface as I second guessed what I was doing. Did Yury really deserve to die?

Yes, Lucinda. Now, end him! the voice shouted in my head.

My hands jerked to snap his neck like he'd done to mine, but at the same time, he lifted his hand and shoved it into the cut he'd made in my stomach. My back arched and head fell back while my blood began to boil.

"What did you do?" I roared.

"Something that would have hurt a lot less if you had stayed still," he grunted, pulling his hand out, covered in blood.

You're such a disappointment, Lucinda. We could have been great, but now, you'll be known as nothing other than a failure, the voice seethed as it fought for control.

Magic swirled around me, teal beginning to intertwine with the black. Yury stood, grabbing me by the back of the neck and turning me around to view Olida's crumpled form on the ground. "You better hope she's still breathing, or I will be the least of your problems. Fight for control, Hulk."

I couldn't see her face as I tried to regain my

composure. My thoughts were still jumbled, and the pull on my magic increased while my strength weakened. After several moments of uncertainty, clarity returned. The darkness was no longer in control, and my previous actions replayed in my head as I tried to get my strength back.

I'd lost power over my own movements. Again. Rage had taken center stage, and I'd pushed Olida away when I'd gotten free, but had it been that hard?

You killed her, and they'll never forgive you. The voice was barely audible as more of my teal magic surrounded me, but I'd heard it, regardless, and the guilt knocked me to my knees as Yury let go of me.

Gods, as much as I hated not being in control of my own body, the feelings assaulting me were almost worse. My eyes and throat burned, but I couldn't make myself check on Olida. I didn't want to know if I had killed her.

"You're going to be a mess for the rest of the day, but it is done. The magic which did not belong to you is gone," Yury said, almost sounding sympathetic for the first time.

I didn't lift my head or respond, but he wasn't having any of that. "You will bleed out if you sit here acting like a child. Get up and save her, then she can try to fix you the rest of the way. Though, I don't think that is possible."

My head jerked up as a surge of willpower filled me, and I glared at him while he smirked down at me. I played right into his hand, but I didn't care. Yury's insult reminded me of what I was capable of, and I stood up. Or at least tried to.

"You gutted me like a fish, asshole," I grunted, grabbing on to the table I'd been strapped to.

He shrugged, helping me stand. "I had to put the spell at your core. You should have stayed still."

My hands were covered in blood, but I was able to walk as I grabbed a towel from the table and pressed it against my stomach. Each step made me wince, my own healing not kicking in, and I hoped like hell that part of me wasn't connected only to the dark magic I'd carried all my life. Mosi had said I was neither light nor dark, so I had to assume normal fae traits might not apply to me.

I bent to the ground without an ounce of grace and nearly fell on top of Olida. Pushing at her shoulder, I rolled her over and watched her chest. The movements were slight, but she was breathing. I sagged against the wall and closed my eyes.

"I'm just going to take a little nap," I murmured as my head lolled to the side.

Yury's chuckle was the last thing I heard as I drifted off, having no idea who I would be when I woke up.

CHAPTER 4

Dreams more vivid than I'd ever remembered were assaulting me on repeat. As hard as I tried to wake up, nothing worked, not even when I'd run toward the cliff during one of them. I was certain I'd died and been stuck in some sort of hell where bits of a life I'd never have were played out, but each memory was cut off at a pivotal moment.

Moments like me almost killing Zephyr but never seeing the sword connect with his body, or seeing Finn in a crisp black suit but not knowing if it was for a funeral or a wedding. Honestly, that one was more of a nightmare, along with seeing Neva's bloodied and broken body but not being strong enough to fix her.

Finally, they ended, and I floated in nothingness for what seemed like endless hours. For the most part, wherever I was stuck was dark, but there were flashes of color I tried to grasp on to and could never keep my hold.

I was alone for the first time in my life. Truly alone.

Even though I'd considered my inner voice still me, I'd never felt on my own while it was inside my head. The voice and strength of its power had pushed me through the hell I'd been through at too young of an age. Even though it also tried to control me, a part of me was thankful for it. Just a small part.

I'd given a lot of thought about what I wanted out of life. As much as I hadn't thought it was possible, I realized I could start over. Not necessarily become a different me, but an improved one.

I still wanted to gut Yury like he had me, but I didn't have the want to kill him. I wanted to tell Finn I accepted the bond, and that I wouldn't fight him anymore. He'd accepted me at my worst and deserved for me to quit fighting what I already knew was inevitable.

I wanted Neva to know how much her friendship had meant to me, even when I did my best to push her away. She'd fought for me and believed in me when nobody else did. There was no way I could repay that, but I'd at least try.

All of those things didn't exactly matter if I couldn't wake up, though.

Another flash of color struck near me like lightning. It was dark blue, almost blending in with the bleakness around me. My arms moved as I tried to swim toward it, but my movements were slowed, like I was treading through sand.

A spark of blue was left over from the strike. It was the

first time that had happened, and I *knew* I had to touch it. Muscles burned in my legs as I kicked like hell, but no matter how hard I tried, my speed never increased.

What felt like hours later, the blip of color was almost gone, but I only had inches to go. Kicking another dozen times, my fingers stretched to touch the light. As they pressed down, nothing happened.

"What the hell?" I grumbled to myself.

Lifting my hand, there wasn't anything left. The spark was gone, and so was my hope. This was my own personal hell.

"Lucinda, come back," a distorted voice echoed around me.

"Get me the hell out of here!" I yelled in return, my body finally growing tired and cold.

Lightning flashed across the sky above me again, the same dark blue color but with a silver outline I hadn't noticed before. Then, it flashed a second time and headed straight for me. I had no will left to get out of the way. I stared at the mesmerizing colors and held my arms out, closing my eyes, accepting my fate.

Warmth filled my core, and I sucked in a breath as my back arched. Fresh air filled my lungs, and I jerked upright when I felt movement at my side. My eyes opened to find Finn sleeping beside me, his arms twitching as if he was dreaming.

My hand settled onto his, and his eyes popped open. "Lucinda," he breathed, chest rising and falling in rapid succession.

"Finnigan." I smirked, holding on tighter when he moved to bring me closer.

His forehead pressed against mine. "I was dreaming of you. I kept calling for you, but you never replied. My magic became uncontrollable searching for you through the bond. Then, I heard you scream… Are you really awake? Is this real?"

His dream sounded a hell of a lot like the flashes of light I saw. Maybe he hadn't been dreaming at all. Our powers worked in ways nobody would ever truly understand, and I wouldn't dismiss the thought, but it didn't matter now. I'd found my way back.

"I'm here, and the darkness is gone. All of it this time." My hand pressed against my chest as magic swirled within me, different than before. I was me, just a fae. Not light or dark. Only uniquely me, and that was okay.

"I thought you'd never wake up," he murmured into my neck.

"I'm not that easy to kill, remember?" I teased, trying to lessen the tension radiating around us.

His upper body shuddered. "There was so much blood. I almost killed Yury for you, but Olida stopped me. She's a lot stronger than she looks."

His hold loosened as I smiled at his words and sat up in the bed, glancing around. We were in the hut Mosi had given us. All of the windows were open, and the salty sea air blew in with the breeze. Glancing down at my attire, I noticed black leggings and an oversized white shirt that looked a lot like the ones Finn enjoyed wearing.

"How long was I out this time?" I was about done with being unconscious.

Finn grimaced. "Three days. All of your wounds healed within the first and everyone expected you to wake when that happened, but nothing we did worked."

"As long as Yury didn't get his unpleasant hands on me again, then I appreciate the efforts. What happened?" I asked.

"Yury and Olida kept the entire plan from us. Even Mosi didn't know what was happening. I've never seen him more furious. And Neva… You'd have been proud. She pinned Yury to the wall with her power and cut off his air supply until Mosi announced you and Olida were still breathing. Then, she punched him in the kidney."

Well, at least everyone else was having fun while I had been in my own personal hell.

"Come on," I said, attempting to remove myself from his lap. "We need to get the others and go back to the castle. No more waiting. This needs to be finished before Zephyr figures out a way to find us. I'm sure the fact that he hasn't isn't for lack of trying."

His brow pinched together, and I could see him overthinking, but it wasn't necessary.

"I'm fine, Finn. There is no darkness left in me. I am thinking for myself, but I am still me—bloodthirsty and all, but in a good way." I winked and paused. "You didn't get that lucky when the dark magic was removed."

Finn cradled my face in his hands, his silver eyes softening. "You have no idea how I see you. How much I admire your strength, and how little it matters to me if you're still bloodthirsty or not." One palm moved to cover my chest. "As long as your heart still beats, you're mine. All of you, no matter how you change."

And that was my undoing.

I'd already known it myself, but I hadn't just wanted to throw the words out there and make a fool out of myself. Finn had given me the perfect opportunity to tell him what I'd been thinking, and I wasn't going to dismiss it.

My hands fisted in his t-shirt as I pulled him closer. "And you're mine."

I heard the hitch in his breath and knew he needed more. Hell, he deserved more after putting up with all my shit.

"Your dream wasn't just a dream, Finn. The bond, magic acting erratically—it was real, even if you were sleeping and I was unconscious. I heard you yell my name once toward the end, and even though I didn't know it was you, I fought like hell to get to your magic. I might have thought whatever it was would end my suffering, but instead, it brought me back to you. You brought me back."

Finn sat up fully, pulling me onto his lap. "I will always bring you back. What we have, what we could have… it's worth fighting for, and I'm not going to let you get away so easily. Neither is our bond."

I smiled. "I know."

He grinned back. "I should be offended you didn't swoon over that, but it just makes me want you more."

"I'm not the type of girl to swoon, ever. I don't like public displays of affection. I will continue to be the most stubborn fae you've ever met. Most importantly, I won't share my feelings all of the time, but it won't change them and the fact that I accept you, Finn. All of it. Including the bond."

His eyes bled charcoal as my words registered. "You are the most incredible being in all the worlds, Lucinda Morrow." Then, he kissed me fiercely, with all of the pent-up emotions I expected.

We'd been through hell, both of us, and we still had more to get through, but I knew Finn would be what kept me grounded. I pushed him until he fell back onto the bed, then I crawled on top of him.

"Show me how much you missed me," I said, removing my clothes with the help of magic before doing the same to him.

His fingers dug into my hips as his hard length twitched beneath me. "I'm going to show you so much more than that."

With those words, I forgot about any earlier need to continue the hunt for Zephyr and only focused on Finn. Something we were both overdue for.

～

HOURS LATER, NIGHT HAD SET IN, AND MY GROWLING stomach had woken me up after I'd fallen back to sleep on Finn's chest. My finger trailed along his ribs as I contemplated leaving him asleep to get some food. I hadn't properly eaten in days, and that was going to stop today.

"Keep touching me like that and I'm going to let you starve," he grumbled, rolling over and getting out of bed.

I followed to do the same, finding a brush on a dresser and using it to get the knots out of my long iridescent strands. "You talk a big game, but you're the one that got out of bed first," I teased, standing in front of a mirror and watching him through the reflection.

His eyes narrowed as I put the brush down and magicked myself some clothes before we got distracted again, then waltzed toward him. My hand splayed over his still-bare chest and my fingers drummed. "Hurry up and get dressed, Finnigan. We have places to be and kings to kill."

He shook his head and laughed. "Yes, ma'am."

I waited at the door for him and, within a minute, we were outside and teleporting to Olida and Mosi's hut. There was light filtering through the door, so I didn't bother to knock when we arrived. I strode in without a worry, unlike the last time I'd been here, and was glad to see the damage from my previous outbursts had already been repaired.

I'd only made it two steps inside before Neva launched herself at me. Her arms wrapped around my neck and feet dangled off the ground for a few seconds until she released me. Her honey eyes narrowed as she shoved me with more force than I expected, but Finn was behind me, preventing me from stumbling too far.

"I told you not to do that again," she fumed.

I reached for her, but she backed up. "Hey, it's not like I knew I was going to be out of commission for several days. Blame the oaf that rammed his fist into my gut."

She smirked. "Oh, I did, and he's still hiding in the forest."

My eyes searched the room. Only Mosi and Olida were present. "Where are Maddox and Ivy?" I asked.

"Ivy wasn't feeling well, so they called it a night earlier," Olida said, bringing a plate of food to me.

"Yury still hasn't fixed her yet?" I sneered.

Finn guided me further into the hut. "She isn't healthy enough. Yury warned if he pulls the poison from her body and she's not strong enough to fight for survival, then she could die anyway."

"Yeah, well, Yury is an idiot. What does Ivy think?" I asked as we stood in the living room and I started to eat the cheese and crackers Olida gave me. My stomach protested the food, but I ignored it and ate as much as I could, knowing I needed it.

"She isn't really saying much," Finn grumbled.

Well, that wasn't going to work for me. Ivy needed to fight her way through the shitstorm she'd been stuck in, and someone needed to push her in the right direction. I had zero problems being that person.

"Who wants to take me to her?" I asked, assuming Finn would volunteer, but Olida beat him to it.

"I know where they are. Let's go and have a chat," she said, grabbing on to my arm.

As Olida moved us back toward the door, Mosi stopped her. "Wait a minute, Mate. We have other matters to discuss."

She huffed. "Too much talking, not enough doing. Lucinda is awake. It's time to take action before there is nothing left of Fae Islands to save."

I wasn't sure what she was talking about, but an idea began forming in my mind. I hated the islands. They were filled with shit childhood memories and were nearly all dead at this point anyway.

"What if we left and sealed the realm? Is that possible?" I asked.

Everyone looked at me with shock, but I couldn't tell if it was because the question was appalling to them, or genius, or a little of both. Either way, I didn't much mind, making me happy that not everything about my personality had changed with the inner darkness gone.

"It's plausible, but getting all of the fae still stuck here to safety without alerting Zephyr would be nearly impossible," Mosi answered. "I won't leave innocents behind to die in this world."

"But it's a good plan B if everything goes to shit, right?" I wasn't stupid enough to believe that Zephyr didn't have plenty of obstacles set in our way of getting to him after all of the days that had passed since infiltrating the castle.

Mosi grimaced. "More like Plan Z, but yes, it's one we can consider at a much later time if necessary."

Olida took my hand. "Well, while you guys worry about plans A through Y, we're going to see Ivy."

Mosi pulled her back once again. "I don't think so. Everyone needs to sit. Ivy is resting. You can see her in the morning."

Neva sat first, which surprised me considering her earlier outburst. I guess it couldn't hurt to hear what Mosi had to say and see Ivy after. The order in which those two things happened wasn't important.

I sat next, then Finn, and Olida sat across from us. Mosi still stood, and I raised a brow at him. "Just waiting on you, oh wise one."

He sighed but took a seat anyway.

"You guys really need a table. The whole pillows-and-ground thing is getting a little old," I added.

Olida laughed. "We're not used to this much company, but I was thinking the same thing earlier today."

Mosi cleared his throat. "Anyway… Let's recap and make sure everyone is on the same page, shall we?"

He glanced around, waiting for an objection. He wouldn't receive one from me. I wanted to make sure I hadn't missed more than what had already been said while I was off in la-la land.

"Very well. Our goal is still to remove Zephyr from his throne. He is continuing to burn the lands until he uncovers where we are hiding. We have weakened his wall by taking out his best asset in Gabriel, plus dozens of his men. Lucinda is free from any control Zephyr might have had on her, but still just as powerful as she was before if what I'm sensing is any indication. Going along with what Maeve said, if we can catch Zephyr in one of his aging fits, he will be easier to kill," Mosi said, and I interrupted.

"I'm not waiting for one of those. Give me the sword, and I can kill him."

All eyes went to me. Disappointment mixed with fear was the vibe I read from each of them.

"Lucinda, you can't have that sword," Finn stated.

I waved my hand at him. "I don't want its power, but I can still use it against Zephyr. I have my own plan for that bastard's death, and it doesn't involve me taking in dark magic. Everyone can get their panties out of their asses now."

"Care to share how this plan of yours will work?" Finn asked.

I drummed my fingers against my knees, wondering if I should. They probably weren't going to like it. The group didn't take risks like I did, but my gut was telling me this was the only way around the king's spell.

We had to fight power with power.

"I'm going to make the not-witch seal the sword so that I can wield it without going all Carrie on you guys. Then, when I drive it into the bastard king's chest, I'll remove the seal."

"And what if it only makes him stronger?" Neva asked.

"It won't."

"How do you know?" she pressed.

I grinned, thinking of my favorite part of the plan. "Because before we seal it, we're going to cover it in the poison we take from Ivy and give him back what he deserves."

osi's eyes closed, and his head rocked back and forth after my announcement. Olida scrambled to his side, gripping his arms tightly as Mosi's movements became erratic.

"What's happening to him?" Finn asked.

Olida's shoulders tensed as she struggled to keep hold of her mate. "He's having a vision. Give it a minute," she replied through gritted teeth.

The rest of us stood and stepped closer, but Olida glared at me when she caught sight of us, and we backed off until Mosi reopened his eyes. They were nearly white and disturbing as hell.

"New paths have emerged. Only one will lead to victory, the others to death. Choose wisely, or all will perish," he murmured, then closed his eyes before his body went lax.

"Well, if that wasn't ominous, then I don't know what is," I sighed.

Olida whispered to Mosi as she lowered him to the ground. "He should come to in a moment and tell us more."

We waited, Neva and Finn more patient than me as I tapped my foot against the wood floor and twisted my hair between my fingers. We didn't have any more hours to waste.

Finally, Mosi began to stir, and Olida helped him sit up. When his eyes opened, they were once again mahogany and he seemed to be back in control.

"Lucinda will wield the sword, but you must remove Maeve from the picture before you act against Zephyr. She will work against us in hopes of Zephyr killing Lucinda before Maeve kills him and takes the throne," Mosi said, staring only at me.

"That wannabe witch isn't powerful enough to take down the king with a few Renegades. She isn't anything to worry about," I replied, not wanting any more delays.

He shook his head. "She wasn't until you provided her with the one thing that she needed to become a formidable opponent to all. Do not underestimate her, Lucinda. Maeve is more than what she appears."

My chin jutted out. "Yeah, well, so am I."

Mosi smiled. "Yes, you are."

Olida turned toward the rest of us. "I think that's enough for tonight. Mosi needs rest after visions, or he's a ripe pain in my ass the following day. Go see Ivy. Tomorrow, we will get Yury to remove the poison and you three can go find Maeve again. No time to waste when there's a tyrant to murder." She winked at me before dismissing us and giving Mosi her full attention.

The three of us left the hut without another word, then gathered outside. Unnatural light illuminated around the wooden door for only a second before the structure went dark to the rest of us.

I glanced up, taking in the full moon above us, and sighed. "Where are Ivy and Maddox?"

"Follow me," Finn said before disappearing.

I grabbed Neva's hand and followed his trail, ending up at one of the smaller huts I remembered seeing when I'd first arrived on the island.

Neva walked up first and lightly tapped with her pointer finger on the bamboo section of the door nearest to us. Shuffling sounded from inside, then a thud, followed by cursing.

Maddox stumbled out, face twisted and holding his elbow. "Stupid coat hook was put on the wall just to torture me." He nodded at me. "Good to see you alive, Lucy."

I grinned and winked. "Wish I could say the same about you."

"Was it too much to hope that she'd be nicer once the dark magic was gone?" he asked Finn.

Finn chuckled. "Hope is a fickle thing."

"Is Ivy awake?" Neva asked.

Maddox shook his head. "I wouldn't have been staggering around in the dark if she was." Then, he tripped out of the doorway, landing face down on the ground.

"The light would have been less disruptive than your stomping," Ivy said, coming to stand in the opening while crossing her arms and smiling at the rest of us. "Come on in, guys."

I stepped over Maddox before he could fully stand. "Gladly."

The hut they were staying in was considerably smaller than Mosi and Olida's, but at least had couches, so I took a seat. Even though I'd been asleep for three days prior, I was still somehow exhausted.

Neva sat next to me on the couch, and Finn sat at my other side while Ivy and Maddox took the loveseat.

"So, what's new?" I asked casually.

Ivy shrugged. "Oh, you know. A little of this and a bit of that."

I leaned forward, taking in her pale skin and the deep purple circles beneath her eyes. "You're growing weaker instead of stronger, Ivy. Why are you waiting for Yury to get that shit out of you?"

Maddox glanced between the two of us. "What are you talking about?"

The poor fairy boy wasn't seeing what was right in front of his face, and I almost felt bad for him. "Ivy?" I raised a brow at her and settled back into the cushions.

Her eyes narrowed, but she didn't scare me. It took me two seconds to see she was hiding something. The others just didn't want to believe it. They were being too easy on her because of whatever hell she'd been through, but that wasn't what Ivy needed.

She huffed and turned toward Maddox, taking his hand. "I'm sorry."

"Sorry for what?" he seethed.

Ivy addressed all of us. "Lucinda is right. Yury could have already healed me, but I didn't let him. And not because I wasn't strong enough like he warned."

Finn and Maddox jumped to their feet, both of them yelling their outrage at the same time. Neva glanced up at me and shook her head.

"Hey, I didn't do anything but state the obvious. It's not my fault all of you refused to acknowledge what was happening," I said.

Neva nodded. "I saw it, but I thought she knew what she was doing, considering she's a healer. I didn't assume she'd just let herself die."

Ivy stood between Finn and Maddox, who were still reprimanding her and demanding answers but not shutting up long enough to let her speak.

"Stop! Both of you," Ivy yelled, power emanating from her palms, and they paused. "Sit back down, and I'll tell you." She heaved the last words out, her actions having taken more energy than she had.

Maddox grumbled and Finn stomped his way back to me, then Ivy took her place again. "I think Mosi was wrong. I was supposed to die in that castle."

Maddox tried to interrupt, but Ivy smacked her hand over his mouth. "Say one more word and you're sleeping in the trees with Yury."

He glared at her but nodded, and she removed her hold.

Ivy continued, "Ever since we arrived back from the castle, I have weakened by the day. My thoughts are jumbled half the time, my movements slower, and my body aches for a relief I don't know how to get. I thought it was just the effects of the magic Gabriel hit me with, but it's been days and I've gotten worse.

"I'm afraid of who I will be once Yury is done with me. I've been nothing but a liability to you all, and I'm tired. I just want it to all be over. Not to say I *want* to die, but seeing what happened to Lucinda made me wonder if removing the poison was really the best choice. I thought I could go back to normal, or the normal I was before being kidnapped. Then, I'd see what happened when Zephyr was killed. I didn't anticipate I'd get worse."

I knew she was leaving out the parts about what Zephyr's abuse had done to her, but I figured I'd called her out on enough already. I'd let her keep those hardships to herself like I once had.

Neva stood and walked to Ivy with her hands out. "May I?" Ivy nodded, then Neva placed her palm over Ivy's forehead and wrapped the other hand around the back of Ivy's head. A soft golden glow illuminated from Neva as she closed her eyes.

Another minute later, Neva backed up, and the color was back in Ivy's face and her eyes brighter. "What did you do?" Ivy asked.

"Just something my mother taught me long ago. It won't last, but I think I know why you're worsening," Neva replied, then glanced back at me. "The shield around the island is blocking the connection Ivy has to Zephyr. Her life is linked to his. It's why she couldn't leave Fae Islands before. Even though she's still within the realm, she's hidden here, and it's affecting her. The sooner the poison comes out, the better."

Ivy's glow was already diminishing as she stood. "I can't believe I didn't put the connection together. But still, I don't see the point."

And maybe I wasn't going to let her have secrets.

"Those are the words of a victim, Ivy. You went through hell, and you're allowed a pity party, but do you really want to be weak? Do you really want to let them win after what they did to you? If your answer is yes, you're not the fae I thought you were and that's damn disappointing."

Ivy floundered for a response as Neva backhanded me in the stomach. "Don't be rude."

I held my hands up. "Hey, I'm still just stating the obvious."

Neva ignored me, turning to Ivy. "I can keep helping you, but your decline will only become more rapid every time I intervene. The choice is still yours."

Maddox was tense by her side as Ivy stood back up and walked to Neva, giving her a hug. "Thank you, but that's not necessary. Lucinda is right. She's an asshole, but I needed to hear her words." She turned toward the rest of us. "Who thinks we should wake up Yury instead of waiting until tomorrow?"

I grinned, surprisingly glad to know I'd made a

difference. "I would love nothing more. That bastard doesn't deserve a moment's rest."

Yes, I was holding a grudge against him, and no, I didn't intend to let it go anytime soon.

Ivy took my arm, and we headed outside with Neva on our tails as the guys complained behind.

"They're going to get us killed," Maddox groaned.

"Yury will murder them, and then we'll die avenging their deaths," Finn added dramatically.

I cast a quick glance behind me. "Quit your whining." Then, I teleported with Ivy and Neva to where I'd last seen Yury during my stint in the trees.

"Hey, you big oaf. Get your ass out here," I called as soon as we appeared in the forest.

The sound of birds flying off was my only reply until Finn and Maddox popped into existence.

"You two are—" Finn started to say, but Yury cut him off.

"Nothing but trouble," the Russian grumbled. "What is it now? Come to say thank you for saving your life?"

I stepped toward him, ready to unleash all of the rage I'd been building since he cut into me, but just when I opened my mouth, realization smacked me in the face. Yury wasn't the problem. The darkness had been. He hadn't handled the situation any different than I would have if I was being honest.

Except, we also had this odd relationship of continuing to poke at each other, so instead of yelling at him or being nice, I went for something in the middle.

"You can have your 'thank you' after you do what you were brought here to do. It's time to fix Ivy. No more waiting. We have places to be and people to kill." My fingers snapped in his face as I fought a grin at his annoyance.

His sneer intensified, scars reflecting off the light of the moon. "Don't tell me what to do, little fae."

I stepped closer to him as Finn tried to pull me back, but it wasn't necessary. "Oh, don't act like you don't enjoy it. Now, let's get moving."

Yury pulsed with magic, and I didn't back away, not even when his power began to burn my skin.

Finally, Yury bowed his head. "Okay, Lucinda. I will remove the poison from your friend."

"Perfect. Your place or mine?" I asked, glad we could quickly come to an agreement.

He grunted. "Mine, unfortunately."

Yury opened a portal and we all stepped through it, appearing in some sort of cave. "Where the hell are we?" Maddox asked, holding Ivy close at his side as the opening closed and a wooden door appeared in its place.

"My house," Yury replied, his back to us as he dug through the drawer of a long oak dresser.

"We all assumed you were sleeping in the trees. Are we still on Mosi's island?" Maddox asked, clarifying his previous question as I glanced around.

The place was a cross between a cave and a cabin, made from what looked like a boulder on one side and wood beams on the other. The ceiling was mostly rock and just tall enough to keep Yury from hitting his head.

The sorcerer's unibrow lowered into a glower. "Do I look like an idiot?"

I choked down a laugh. "Can I please answer that?"

Everyone echoed, "No." Fun ruiners.

"So, we're in your secret lair somewhere on Mosi's island. Super. But now I can see why you kept the socks-with-sandals fashion statement. You weren't actually living in the trees," I commented.

Finn pinched the bridge of his nose. "Lucinda, please keep your thoughts to yourself. For Ivy's sake."

I glanced at his sister, and she grinned. "I don't mind it. Best entertainment I've had in weeks." A shadow fell over her eyes as a memory from her time in the castle likely smacked her in the face. I'd seen the same expression in my own reflection for months after I'd begun training with Gabriel years ago.

Yury turned around with a dagger in one hand and a bottle of crimson liquid in the other.

I put my hand up. "No. You're banned from using sharp objects on people. You have shit bedside manners."

He grunted. "I never agreed to be nice, just to save the girl. Now, move out of my way before I stab you again."

"Hurt her like you did me, and you're going to have a lot of upset people in your cave," I sneered, no longer joking with him.

"Calm down, Hulk. I just need a few drops of her blood," Yury replied as he shouldered his way past me.

"Right," I muttered while I turned around to watch. "Besides some of her blood, how are you going to remove the poison?"

Yury pointed at Ivy and then toward a chair against the rock wall instead of answering me. "Sit."

"I'm not a dog," Ivy replied as Maddox guided her toward the seat, whispering something in her ear that made her glare at him.

"Yeah, yeah. All you women, so strong and powerful. Yet, you all need my help," Yury droned before using his teeth to rip the cork from the bottle, shoving it at Ivy. "Drink."

Ivy took the potion, then glanced at me.

"Before she drinks that, how about you tell us what you're doing?" I asked again since he hadn't answered before.

Yury groaned. "I am doing my job. One I won't explain. Just stay out of my way and Ivy will be fine."

Oh, he was lucky I was trying to turn over a new leaf, because I really wanted to threaten and yell at him. Instead, I held my tongue as he continued gathering items to place by Ivy.

With Maddox's encouragement and my lack of objection, Ivy drank the potion, and we all watched in anticipation.

Ivy gulped the liquid down in two drinks. Then, Yury snatched her hands as Ivy's body stiffened. I flinched to react, but Finn stopped me even as Yury slashed across both of Ivy's palms.

Then, black ooze poured from Ivy's mouth and hands. I clawed against Finn's relentless hold, but he didn't release me, and all my previous reasoning fled as Ivy's body began to quake.

CHAPTER 6

*Y*ury shot his arm out before I could touch him, his gorilla-sized hands wrapped around my neck and squeezing just enough that he had my attention.

"Stop or you will kill her," he grunted, never taking his eyes away from Ivy and using the dagger in his other hand to lure in the black poison escaping from Ivy.

"If you'd have answered me when I asked what you planned to do, I might not have tried to attack you." I spat the words at his back.

Without looking at me still, Yury grunted and released his hold on me. "Sure."

Maybe he was right, and I'd have been furious either way, but we'd never know. All that mattered now was that he saved Ivy. Finn was right behind me, holding on to my waist, likely so I didn't retaliate against Yury again, but it wasn't necessary as long as Ivy didn't get worse.

Ivy's head lolled to the side and while her eyes were still open, she wasn't coherent. Maddox took a step forward, but Neva intercepted him before he could interfere like I almost had.

I stopped paying them any attention as Yury continued to move the dagger in a circular motion around Ivy's face and then both of her hands.

When everyone was staying put again, Neva moved to stand beside me. Suffocating tension rolled off both of us in waves. I knew I wanted to stop living in fear and stop keeping people at a distance, but maybe I needed to rethink that. Caring caused a whole new ache in my chest that had never been there before.

Blood pooled beneath Ivy into two small pots I hadn't noticed before. When the blade Yury held was nearly obsidian, he dipped it into one of the pots, then resumed his circular movements. He repeated this process several times until the oozing stopped.

By the time Yury was done, Ivy appeared like a murder victim with blood splattered all over her and death in her eyes. I wasn't sure Yury had helped, but nobody else voiced their concerns, so I kept my composure.

"Do not touch her." Yury picked up the pots and carried them to a circle of rocks near the boulder wall. With a snap of his fingers, flames erupted, and he moved to empty the contents into the fire.

"Wait!" I called out. "I need one of those buckets."

Yury paused, cocking his head to the side. "Why?"

"To kill Zephyr. Who has the sword?" I asked to anyone who might know.

Yury stood up, staring at Neva and Finn. "No."

Neva sighed. "She doesn't want the dark magic. The sword will be a decoy of sorts."

"How?" Yury asked, still holding the buckets precariously over the fire.

"I want you to poison the sword with whatever is in those pots, and then seal it so only I can break it, but not until the blade is submerged in Zephyr's chest cavity," I answered.

Yury glanced between the three of us as Maddox began to protest. "If you could figure that out later, that would be great. Ivy's not waking up."

With measured steps, Yury set one of the buckets on a side table. "Touch that and the poison will be the least of your worries," he threatened before turning to carefully pour the remainder of poisoned blood over the fire. Instead of the embers dying out from the liquid, they turned shadowy and smoke wafted around the room.

"Uh, should we be concerned with that?" I asked, covering my mouth with my shirt.

When Yury ignored me, Neva used her own magic to keep the smoke on the other side of the room as Finn pulled me further back. Maddox however was still at Ivy's side, his hand hovering over her face. "Some urgency would be nice considering she's barely breathing," he seethed.

Yury's movements didn't quicken as he returned and stood over Ivy. The sorcerer pulled another vial from his pocket and tilted her head back before forcing her mouth open. Maddox began to object, and Yury punched him in the chest, sending Maddox flying six feet in the opposite direction.

"My patience is gone. If anyone else wants to interrupt my work, you get hit," he grumbled while pouring the amber liquid down Ivy's throat.

"Seriously. Should we be concerned? He might be a beast, but we can take him," I said to Finn when we couldn't see Ivy around Yury's massive form.

"Probably, but Mosi trusts him or Yury wouldn't still be on the island. Just refrain from trying to kill the Russian a little bit longer," Finn replied as he cast a quick glance at Maddox before refocusing on Ivy again.

Coughing sounded from across the room as Neva rejoined us and Yury moved out of the way so we could see Ivy again. "She lives. Now, go."

"You really need to work on your hospitality skills, Not Witch. People might like you more," I said as we rushed forward.

He muttered something about unwanted guests in his house as he began dealing with the black flames that still flickered against the rock wall, no longer putting off noxious smoke.

Ivy continued coughing until she was gagging, then promptly threw up on the floor, just missing Finn's boots. Maddox grabbed on to her strawberry-blonde locks and held them back as her stomach emptied and the dry heaving took over.

When she finally lifted her head up, red splotches covered her face, but her green eyes were bright, and she was grinning from ear to ear. "It's gone. The poison is really gone."

Before anyone could say anything, she launched out of the chair, pushing past me and Finn with a disgruntled Maddox trailing right behind her. Yury hadn't even turned all the way around when Ivy threw herself at him, wrapping her arms around his waist.

"Thank you. Thank you so much," she cried into his side.

Yury glared at me, a panic in his eyes I'd yet to see as he held his arms as far from Ivy as they could go. "Get this thing off me." He twisted several times, but Ivy didn't let go until Maddox pried her hands away.

I smirked at the oaf. "Did I forget to tell you she was a hugger? My bad."

"Out. Now. All of you," he snarled, pointing toward the door, then shook his head. "Wait. No, you need to use a portal."

"We're perfectly capable of teleporting," I said with a sigh.

Neva's soft laugh sounded. "He doesn't want us to go out that door and figure out where this place is."

I darted for the exit, my fingers reaching for the handle, but not quite making it as the brass disappeared and trees took its place through a portal opening.

"Have it your way, Not Witch. We'll be seeing you.

I'm assuming since no one replied before that you have the sword. We need to take care of one more annoyance, and then I'm going to need it, so your job isn't done yet," I said with a sweet smile, jumping through the opening and appearing right where we'd been taken from before.

If Yury responded, I didn't hear his reply as the others followed after me and the portal closed before we could even blow him kisses goodbye.

Ivy was bouncing on her toes, and I hadn't seen her this excited since I first appeared on their farm. She started passing out hugs and stopped when she got to me, holding my elbows. "Just this once?" she begged.

"Fine, but make it quick," I groaned.

She laughed in my ear. "You know, you're pretty much my sister now. Maddox told me about you and Finn. You're not getting rid of me. So, you might as well get over your aversion to hugs."

Using both hands, I pulled her off me, holding her a foot away. "Ivy, I will hide in the deepest of oceans for a thousand years before I like hugs."

"Good thing I'm patient, huh?" She patted both of my hands before bouncing back to Maddox, holding him around the waist. "See everyone tomorrow!" Then, they disappeared.

"Well, as exciting as this day has been, I'm ready for it to be over. I'll be in my pocket realm, but just call if you need me," Neva said with a wave and shimmered out of appearance.

Finn grabbed my hand, and the air was pulled from

my lungs as he teleported us back to the hut without asking. "A little eager to be back in bed?" I teased.

His face flushed. "Possibly."

"Given we have a fae-witch to hunt tomorrow, we should probably take advantage of what little time we have to ourselves," I said, already removing my clothes with slow and precise movements as Finn's heated gaze traveled along every inch of skin I exposed.

He leaned back on the bed, beckoning me forward. "With that, I won't argue."

JUST AS THE SUN CRESTED INTO THE DARK SKY, I WAS OUT of bed and ready to go for the day. Even with Finn distracting me, Maeve hadn't been far from my mind. The bitch had tried to get us killed. The darkness within me was gone, but I didn't need it there to feel immense anger over what she had done. She was going to get what she deserved.

"I can feel you thinking from across the room. Don't worry. We're going to find her," Finn said, appearing behind me as I stared out the window. Little did he know, worry was the least of my emotions.

"I didn't mean to wake you. I was at least going to wait until the sun was above the trees before doing so," I replied.

He laughed. "Sleep isn't as appealing without a warm body next to me. Now, let's go check in with the others and see who's coming with us on our hunt."

Glancing back, I saw Finn was already dressed, and I wasted no time heading out the door. The morning air was crisp, and I tugged my jacket close as I listened for noise but found none. A part of me missed the commotion of LA, and an even bigger part missed my car Black Widow, but there was something calming about Mosi's island that I hadn't expected to find.

While I still had no intentions of staying within the fae realm permanently, I wasn't as hateful toward the place as I once had been. Having the darkness stripped from me probably had a lot to do with it, but that wasn't something I cared to overthink as we arrived in front of Mosi and Olida's hut.

Their door was cracked open, and the smell of fresh baked bread wafted outside, making me rush toward the door.

Olida was standing in their small kitchen, just slicing into a new loaf as I entered. She wore a purple apron that matched her eyes and smiled up at me as she flicked her lengthy grey hair back. "Good morning, Lucinda." Then, she nodded behind me. "Finn. Hungry?"

"Famished," I sighed, snatching the first two pieces she'd already cut.

She leaned closer to me and not-so-quietly said, "Tends to happen when you spend all your free time indoors with your mate."

I winked at her, shoving the piece of bread into my mouth and holding in a moan as the lemony flavors melted against my tongue. There was no need to give the spunky fae any further ammunition to talk about my sex life.

Neva came in behind us as Finn grabbed some breakfast as well. "Where's Ivy and Maddox?" she asked.

Mosi landed with a thud in the living room, having jumped from their loft above. "They're not coming."

"Why?" Finn questioned suspiciously.

Olida threw a piece of bread at her mate. "You're banned from talking." Then, she stepped toward Finn. "Your sister is fine, but she is not ready for a fight. Maddox would only be distracted by trying to keep her safe and it would put you all at risk instead of helping."

"So, why can't Maddox come on his own?" I asked.

"Even though Ivy and Maddox are not true mates, their love for each other runs deep. Maddox will come if you ask him to, but it's not necessary. You'll have help when the time comes, should you need it," Olida said as she got back to slicing.

I hadn't thought about Ivy and Maddox not being mates. Gods, that would suck if one of them met theirs, but I guess if it worked for everyone else like it did me and Finn, they'd never know unless they had sex with the other person. Maybe it wasn't such a risk after all.

"Where will this extra help come from, and when can we leave?" I asked, distracting myself from the uncomfortable direction of my thoughts.

"You can leave as soon as you'd like. As for the help, well, that could be from two different sources, but you'll know when it happens," Mosi said, picking up the bread that had been thrown at him from the ground, then eating it without a second thought.

I shoved the rest of my food in my mouth and wiped my hands against my dark-wash jeans before reaching back to the door. "Well, that sounds promising. Let's go then." My palm barely pressed against the wood before we were called back.

"Mosi, if you're about to tell me there's something else we have to do before I get to kill Maeve, I'm not going to be very happy with you," I said calmly as magic sparked around me.

He held his hands up. "I was just going to let you know she isn't in the same house she was before and remind you to be careful. Remember, Maeve's more powerful than she was last time you saw her. Do not for one moment underestimate her."

"Got it. Help may or may not come from mysterious sources, find and kill Maeve so we don't fail at killing Zephyr, and watch out for her new powers." I pushed the door open before he could say anything else.

It was time to remove one last obstacle from our path back to Zephyr.

Given that Mosi had let us know Maeve was no longer on North Island, or at least not in the same house, I'd already decided the first place we would go. Hopefully, it would prove to be as helpful as it was the last time we were there.

"Let's head to South Island and find Ash. I don't want to spend all day figuring out which island the half-breed has been tainting since we parted, and he used the trees to find her somehow last time," I said.

"That's a better idea than me trying to track her magic from before," Neva replied.

I raised a brow. "You can do that?"

She shrugged while tying her hair back and stepping closer to me without answering. Whatever. Neva could have her secrets. It only made me like her more. Most of the time.

Without waiting for permission, I reached out and grabbed hold of Neva's shoulder, then took Finn's hand before teleporting the three of us to South Island. The moment we appeared on the beach, death smacked me in the face, and I tried to take in what I was seeing without losing my shit.

My hold tightened on Neva's shoulder as Finn stepped forward, letting go of my hand. I wanted to follow him, but I was frozen in agony. The dying trees nearest to the beach were blown over, roots ripped from the ground, and not a single leaf remained on the branches we could see.

Color had been wiped from everything, and not one tree still lived. The likelihood of Ash still being there didn't seem high. My hope was that if he'd been there when the destruction happened, he hadn't been foolish enough to stay. He was too young to fight against Zephyr's men, no matter how special his powers were.

Neva's hand rested on top of mine. "It's okay, Lucinda."

"No. No, it's not." I stomped toward the trees, letting my anger replace the worry and not knowing my intentions, but needing to be closer to the destruction.

I fell to my knees, holding on to the roots, searching for any amount of life within them. I'd never been drawn to nature, never cared about pollution or global warming. Hell, I'd demolished half a forest just before I left LA, but this... these trees uprooted likely because an egotistical king was throwing a fit. I just couldn't ignore it any longer.

Maybe it was the lack of darkness within me, or

maybe it was just that I'd changed my outlook since the last time we'd been there. Either way, I was hurting for these trees, and the need for vengeance filled my soul.

Magic pulled deep from my core and pulsed from my hands as I kneeled over the roots. *Heal,* I thought over and over again. Ash had said I would save the trees. Even if I hadn't believed him then, I had to try now.

"Lucinda," Finn said my name. I ignored him, focusing on my task, but apparently, he wasn't okay with that.

Power licked at my back, heating my skin until I began to sweat and distracting me from whatever I was attempting to do.

My hold slipped from the roots, and I spun around with my wings out, using the magic still flowing from my hands to propel me forward. Much to my surprise, it wasn't Finn attacking me. It was Neva.

The shock halted me as I cocked my head to the side, not understanding what was happening.

"Lucinda, get control of yourself," she scolded as Finn stepped cautiously toward me.

"I. Am. In. Control," I ground out.

She shook her head. "No, you're emotional. Something you're not used to and dangerous coming from someone with your amount of power. Now, calm down before I have to force you."

Her heat only increased as I glared at her. To think, I was proud of her for finally showing her true self. Now,

I just wanted to murder her. Figuratively, of course, and mostly because I knew she was right.

Before I could attempt to do as she asked and apologize for snapping at her, Ash appeared between us, emerald gossamer wings out and tears in his eyes. "Lucinda, you came."

"What happened here?" I asked.

"King Zephyr. He came looking for you. He's been searching everywhere for all of you the last few days. Burning lands, tearing down buildings, cutting off water supply. Nothing is sacred to him any longer." Ash paused, taking a deep breath. "He is killing our home, and I've nearly failed the trees."

The fae—no longer a small boy but more of a fully grown teen who was still too soft around the edges for this kind of life—freely wept in front of us, his head hanging low and hands covering his face as his shoulders shook. It was the saddest sight I'd ever seen.

The sorrow around us only increased as each of us took another moment to take in the island. Ash didn't appear to be calming down, so I went to him. My hand settled on his arm and flinched at the power simmering beneath the surface of his skin.

His eyes met mine, filled with tears. "You have to help them, Lucinda."

Ash's words, while so simple, packed a punch of emotion I wasn't prepared for. His hand covered mine as he pleaded with me, and I felt a connection to him that had me wanting to protect him, no matter the cost.

As his anguish became mine, a single tear fell from my eye for the first time since I was a child.

Finn stepped to my side and brushed his thumb across my cheek, wiping the stray tear away before turning to Ash. "What can we do?"

My first instinct was to find Zephyr and make him pay, but we had to be smarter than him. Think with our heads and react as he had clearly been doing.

Ash straightened, wiping away his own tears. "I need Lucinda to save the trees."

"I tried. It didn't work." I kept my tone even, trying to keep any further fragile emotions from rising within me. I couldn't afford to be weak when we were hunting Maeve. Mosi's warnings were not forgotten, and letting Ash's reactions get to me wouldn't help any of us.

"One tree still lives. Please come with me," he begged, reaching to hold both of my hands. "Time is almost gone."

My eyes met Finn's, and he nodded. "If she goes, we all go."

Ash beamed with excitement. "Yes, yes. Follow us."

Before anyone could object, Ash teleported from the beach with me in tow. When we reappeared, I heard the echoes of Finn's roar reach us. "You probably shouldn't have done that," I said to Ash, moving to stand in front of him right as Finn appeared.

His jaw was tense as he stared above my head at Ash.

I stepped toward Finn. "At least it wasn't me that took off on you this time," I joked, using humor to lighten the tension as I so often liked to do, and Finn met my stare.

"Sorry, it's just been a long few days. The bond… it's hard to control sometimes," he muttered, grabbing on to me and pulling me close.

"I know." I squeezed him back as Neva appeared behind us, ending the brief moment with Finn. I let him go and turned back to Ash. "So, where is this tree?"

Glancing around, I saw we were near the dried-up creek bed Finn had shown me the first time we were on this island. The trees around us weren't blown over like the others at the beach. Still, none of them were showing any signs of life.

Ash hesitantly walked by Finn and placed his hand on a trunk wider than the rest, covered in smooth madrone bark with marring in the bark that was faded and likely years old. The branches were thick, but empty of leaves.

"This is the only one you need to save," he murmured reverently. His long chestnut hair fell over his face as his forehead pressed against the tree and wings vibrated at his back.

"Are you sure about that?" I asked, not sensing any trace of life around us.

He nodded, fingers clenching over the bark. "This is the mother tree. I have watched over her since I was a toddler. She has cared for me as I grew, taught me all I know, and kept me safe. She is dying, but she is not dead."

"What am I supposed to do? I used my magic down

at the beach and nothing happened," I said, wondering if I'd messed up somehow and sent any sort of beacon out to Zephyr or his men by doing so.

Yury had shielded our magical presence, but I'd never confirmed if that included when we actually used our magic.

"You don't know?" he asked, eyes wide and voice quivering.

I narrowed my eyes at him. "Of course, I don't. Why would I know?"

"Because you're Lucinda Morrow," Ash said, as if that was enough.

I glanced at Finn, unsure of what I was supposed to do. We needed Ash's help—more accurately, the trees—to find Maeve in a timely manner, but they were all dead except one, and I had no idea how to fix them.

Finn nudged me forward. "Just touch it and see what happens."

Well, that was helpful.

I sighed as Ash moved out of the way, face still twisted with concern. "Be gentle with her. She feels like we do, and she's been suffering for days as her children died," he whispered as my hand hovered above the trunk.

My arms shook as I closed the gap between myself and the tree. My palm connected, and a pulse of magic grabbed on to my hand, forming a bond between me and the tree, almost like it had when I touched Ash. Except this was so much more. My forehead pressed against the smooth bark as my muscles relaxed. I was calmer than I'd been in my entire life.

I closed my eyes as my wings spread out and wrapped around the tree, helping to hold me up. Harsh whispers sounded from behind me, but I blocked them out and drew on the warmth from the tree.

"Hello, Lucinda Morrow," a woman's voice said.

"Hmm." Words were lost on me as I grabbed on to the peacefulness like a lifeline. Swirls of blues and greens drifted through my mind like clouds. I'd never known such a feeling. Safety, love, purity. It was addicting, and I wanted all of it.

"And you can have all of it, but first, I need you to help me," the woman added.

"How?" I asked.

"I need you to heal my children through me. I am not strong enough to do this on my own after what the king has done to our lands. The dark magic he uses has poisoned me, and I will die soon without your help," she answered.

At mention of the king, my shoulders stiffened. "How did he do this?"

The woman's voice sighed. "The king is a selfish man. The *hows* and *whys* do not matter, though. We are running out of time. What you feel within me is my soul, but it is dying. Ash has done all he can, and now it is your turn."

"I don't know how," I said, unashamed of my incompetence. I'd healed Maddox, Finn, and Ivy, but I didn't know what I'd done in order to do so. None of those experiences would help me with the trees.

"You are in your purest form now without outside influence—your true self. Draw on that like you did on the beach, but don't do so because you're angry. Do so from your heart, Lucinda. The king might have tainted your greatness at one time, but he no longer has control over you. Find who you are and embrace it."

A sour taste filled my mouth as the peace I'd latched on to was corrupted with memories of the past.

Zephyr pretending to save me and then taking away my childhood. Zephyr burning my favorite doll. Gabriel beating me for days on end until I quit crying when he whipped me. The darkness had been my only friend through it all, and now that was gone.

I had been so sure when I'd woken back up that I knew what I wanted, that I was done being afraid, but this tree was pulling thoughts from me I'd hoped would remain buried.

I might have been in my purest form and knew what I wanted, but I was still afraid of taking it and believing everything would be okay.

I had Finn, but how could I really have him when I didn't know who I was anymore?

I'd always been what everyone else wanted: Zephyr, Gabriel, the darkness. They'd all ruled me for years, and even when I was gone from the island, I'd never truly been free from their terrors.

My shoulders shook as every pain, every loss, and every action swirled within me. With each tear shed, I prayed to the Gods that they would take the other memories from me and allow me to forget the past that had broken me.

"You're not broken, Lucinda. You're powerful and spirited. You will get through this and find yourself, but in order to be born anew, you have to accept all of who you are. You have hidden behind the horrors of your past, using it as an armor. If you wish to move beyond all of that, then you must forgive yourself for the things you've done. Accept that you are a good person with pure intentions. Accept that you are worthy of the devotion your mate provides you."

My hair stuck to my wet cheeks, and I tried to deny her words. I wasn't a good person. I'd killed people, a decent amount that were likely innocent. I made selfish choices. I did what I wanted no matter the consequences, even after I'd gotten free of the king's rule.

It didn't matter that I wanted Finn and he wanted me. Beneath it all, I knew I didn't deserve him after what I'd done. I knew I'd do something to push him away, because being selfish was easier than allowing myself to truly care with my whole heart.

Warmth settled over me like a soft blanket. "I am the mother to the trees and nature. I am the first to grow on these islands, and I will be the last. I have seen many fae in my time, Lucinda. The fates would not have blessed you with the feathered wings on your back and the power to choose your destiny if they did not believe in you."

With my forehead still pressed against the bark and palms locked onto the trunk, I had tears and snot running down my face. I imagined it was quite the sight, but I wasn't bothered by it, because the more I cried, the more she spoke, and the clearer my thoughts became.

"How am I free to choose my destiny? I've had everything chosen for me. My mate, these powers, the pressure to save everyone. How is any of this my choice?" I asked.

"I don't for one second believe that the powerful Lucinda Morrow didn't choose her mate. You had every opportunity to reject him, did you not?" Her voice was stern and reprimanding.

Technically, she was right. I could have stopped us from having sex the first time. I could have not repeated the same action over and over again after the truth really set in, but I'd chosen to not let him go, to allow the parts of him in that made me want to be a better person.

"You've had a choice this entire time, Lucinda. Even when the darkness took residence within you, your heart has always been stronger," she said.

I wasn't sure how this tree spirit had ripped me open from the inside out, especially since it was supposed to be me saving her, but she'd shown me my true fears. More importantly, she'd given me the courage to move through them.

"Who are you?" I asked as acceptance flooded through me.

"I am the mother tree. I am the purest form of original power that exists in this realm. If you need a name, you may call me Maia."

Her power waned as I squeezed tighter. "Thank you, Maia."

"You're welcome, Lucinda." Her voice sounded far away, and the warmth I'd greedily taken from her was replaced by the cold.

"Maia, how do I heal you?" I asked as panic clawed its way up my chest. Once again, I'd been selfish. I'd thrown my own pity party, and she'd comforted me while she was the one dying.

There was no response from her, but I was still locked onto the tree, which I took to mean she was in there somewhere. A renewed sense of determination filled me as my magic grew to new levels.

I wouldn't give up until I got her back.

CHAPTER 8

$\mathcal{A}$s I held on to the trunk of the mother tree, I tried to figure out how the hell I was supposed to save her. Instead of allowing fury in like usual, I focused on the warmth she'd provided me, the comfort I craved, and the peace the rest of the world deserved.

The longer I did that, the more power built within me, but none of it flowed freely from me to Maia, no matter how hard I pushed.

The colorful swirls still floated through my mind as I searched for answers, reminding me of all the things I'd either disregarded or had never been able to believe.

Somewhere along the way, I'd forgotten who I was. Forgotten the woman inside me that I needed to love first before anything else. She was scarred, but she was worthy.

That's who I was. Scarred yet worthy.

The world would not beat me.

Fear would not dictate my happiness.

The king would not rule me.

I was Lucinda Morrow, and I was in control of my destiny.

Power burst from me in a single blast that rocked my core so harshly that I thought I would end up destroying Maia instead of saving her. But, as I focused on holding tight to the tree, the blue and green cloud-like swirls around me mixed with a dark magic. The old me would have been drawn to it, but I recoiled now.

My hold loosened on the trunk, but I remembered what the mother tree had said before. She was being poisoned with Zephyr's use of dark magic as he sought to destroy everything in his path to find me. I'd only just gotten rid of the power that didn't belong inside me, but none of that mattered. Yury could do his magic on me again. I would do whatever it took to save Maia.

I pulled on the darkness, calling it toward me where I floated in the clouds. The closer the power got to me, the more it accelerated until it pierced my chest and I screamed out in pain.

For the first time since I entered the mother tree's mind, or wherever I was, I felt the presence of others. Hands wrapped around my waist, and as I pulled the dark magic from Maia, someone else was taking it from me.

The bond between me and Finn ebbed and flowed, so I assumed he was the one assisting in whatever was happening. I wanted to stop him. He'd already taken on traces of the poison from Ivy—he didn't need this, too

—but I was frozen in place as the coldness of evil seeped through my chest and out my back.

Accepting that I couldn't stop whatever was happening, I focused on what my eyes could see. The greens and blues turned teal like my own magic while black streaks still barreled their way toward me in a never-ending cycle.

Power struck every few feet like lightning along the pale blue background before splintering out like roots beneath the dirt. The strikes of magic reminded me of when I'd been in the nothingness before, and I knew for sure that Finn was the one helping me save the mother tree.

I continued to push, giving the tree everything I had. As my shoulders began to sag, heat seeped into them, offering a renewed energy source that I greedily took from and gave back to the trees.

"You're doing it, Lucinda. You've accepted your true self," Maia whispered.

No reply left my lips for fear I would break concentration and ruin the connection. I pressed harder, taking and giving all that I could as my breathing labored and my heart raced from her encouragement. Her words and power had given me something I'd never known before: faith.

I'd always said I loved who I was, but that had been a lie. A way to convince myself that hiding behind my pain was better than facing it. I'd done that until Finn Barlow marched into my life and challenged me to face my past demons.

As the inky darkness left the world I'd been floating in, strength zapped out of me, and my hold around the trunk loosened until I collapsed onto the ground, my connection to the tree broken.

Shadows moved above me, and voices called my name, but I ignored them, searching for Maia's presence.

I'm here, Lucinda, she said, but this time in my mind. We were no longer inside her world, and I was mentally present back on the island. I tried not to panic about the chaos that I sensed around me until I knew Maia was healed.

Did it work? Will you live? I asked.

Yes, but more importantly, so will you. By coming back to the fae realm, you have chosen a hard path for yourself. You've yet to face the worst of it, I'm afraid, but you will endure, Lucinda. You just had to have faith in yourself, and now you do. King Zephyr tried to take that from you. Don't let him do it a second time.

I won't, I said confidently.

I know you did not come here to save me. You seek answers, yes? she asked.

Yes, I need to know where Maeve is hiding. Mosi believes she will be trouble for us if we don't remove her from the picture before we face Zephyr.

The fae-witch wishes for things that don't belong to her. Mosi is wise with his words, and you're smart to heed them. You'll find Maeve on a tourist island. Her magic fills the sands as she pulls from life that is not hers to take. Be careful, Lucinda.

With her final warning, my body jolted, and my eyes opened to see Neva kneeling over me. I smiled up at her, but she didn't return the grin. "What's wrong?" I asked.

Neva's lips thinned as tears fought to fall from her honey eyes. "You were stuck to that tree for nearly three hours, Lucinda. I tried to get Finn to stay away, but he didn't listen."

I was up within an instant and searching for my mate, but I didn't see him until I practically threw Neva out of my way. He was lying behind her on the ground, one hand wrapped around an exposed root of the mother tree and the rest of him twisted, as if he'd been thrashing around on the ground.

"It's the darkness," Neva whispered. "It's back."

"Well, it's not here to stay," I snarled, grabbing hold of Finn, but he wouldn't let go of the roots.

Give me my mate, I demanded inside my head, hoping Maia was still linked to me somehow.

There was no response, and I grew impatient.

My wings expanded, and I pulled a feather out, acting purely on instinct and remembering what Yury had done to Ivy.

Since I couldn't get to his left palm, I sliced his forearms instead with my hardened feather and didn't let the blood distract me.

"Should you move away from the mother tree?" Ash asked, getting too close to my personal space.

Neva said something to him that I didn't catch, but he backed off, and I continued trying to save my mate.

I wasn't a witch, and didn't know anything about breaking spells, but from what I'd seen, the dark magic wasn't a spell at all. It was just poison, one I hoped could be removed without killing Finn, because I was about to draw blood from him until he woke up.

Neva reached for me as magic swirled within my hands. "Are you sure this is a good idea?" she asked.

"Do you have anything better? Because I'm pretty sure he's dying right now, Neva, and you don't want to know me if he does," I replied calmly.

I'd only just accepted who I was, but I knew without a doubt that I'd revert back to someone even worse than before if I lost Finn. He kept me grounded. He made me think twice instead of acting first. I couldn't let him die.

"Let me help," she said, and I didn't object.

Neva kneeled next to me and grabbed on to Finn's arms while I sat idly by, not knowing how to help. I wanted to call on his darkness like I'd done so often to mine, except I had no connection to this magic. There were no threads to pull on, nothing tangible to grasp and take from my mate.

"Don't try to kill me for what happens next," Neva said, then acted before I could object.

Her small hands wrapped around the wounds I'd made on Finn's forearms, and blood oozed between her fingers as she squeezed. Power glowed around them so hot that I inched back. Well, until I saw what she did next.

Neva's lips closed around Finn's, shocking the hell

out of me. My initial thoughts were dark, but I reminded myself that Neva was my friend—the truest one I'd ever had—and I needed to trust her. Emotions warred within me as I refrained from interfering and helplessly watched from the side.

Ash joined me, grabbing hold of my hand and offering comfort. His cool touch moved through my arm as he pointed. "She's giving him light magic. Look closer."

As the last of my darker emotions cleared from my vision, I did my best to do as Ash suggested. Amber sparks of magic flickered around Neva's lips that weren't actually kissing Finn like my brain had first thought. She was more so giving him mouth-to-mouth as she squeezed tighter on Finn's arms where I'd cut.

Another minute passed as I struggled to maintain my composure. The mate bond was raging within my body, but I continued to remind myself that this was Neva helping Finn. They were the two most important people in this world to me. By continuing to do so, I managed to stay back as Neva's magic moved from Finn's mouth to the cuts I'd made.

His blood turned from red to an ashy grey as his body began to thrash under Neva's slight frame.

"What's happening?" I hissed, digging my fingers into my legs as I refrained from going to Finn and getting in the way.

"It's the dark magic. It doesn't want to leave his body." She grunted, growing more tired by the second based on breaths she was struggling to take.

"Well, I'm happy to serve its eviction notice." Teal magic swirled around me and inched closer to Finn's body as I hoped Neva would tell me I could help somehow instead of sitting here helpless.

"You can't help, Lucy. The magic will want somewhere to go, and it can't be you," Neva replied.

Before I could respond, a tree branch pushed me back several feet and wind pressed down on me as Ash rejoined me. He was grinning, and I was not happy. My hands planted onto the dirt ground, stopping me from moving any further back.

The branches from the mother tree shook as if she was laughing at me. I glared at the tree trunk, fighting between being glad Maia seemed to be okay and furious that she'd pushed me back when I'd been doing fine at letting Neva do her thing.

"Your friend needs you out of the way. Mother Tree was just helping," Ash said innocently.

"Yeah, I'm sure she was," I replied with a sigh.

As I closed my eyes in an attempt to reach Finn through our bond, Ash's hands grabbed my shoulders and jerked me around. "Look."

An inky cloud of dark magic floated above Neva, but she was surrounded by her own power that it couldn't pierce through. Next, it came floating toward me and Ash. I readied myself for the impact, unafraid of whatever it might mean for me considering I'd spent my whole life with dark magic in me.

Except before anything could happen, Ash was beside me twisting his hands around until a wind funnel formed and he sucked the darkness in. I watched carefully as he walked away from me until he had a clear view of the sky with no tree branches obstructing him and thrust his hands into the sky.

The wind funnel shot into the sky, taking the dark magic with it, and disappeared within mere seconds. When I turned around, Neva was checking Finn's vitals and I hurried back to his side.

She was done by the time I kneeled next to him, shaking his shoulders. "Come on, Finnigan. I need you to wake up now before I kill you myself for leaving me."

With eyes still closed, he smirked. "I used to hate that name, but it's growing on me now," he murmured.

I shoved his chest gently. "Really? You almost died and that's the first thing you say?"

His grin widened and eyes opened as he grabbed on to my arms and pulled me on top of him. "You are perfect." Then, he kissed me like it could be the last time.

Finn's actions and words caught me off guard, so it took me a moment to kiss him back properly. Then, I remembered we weren't alone and pulled back. "We should continue this later."

"Unfortunately, you're right." There was a sparkle in his eyes I'd never seen before.

"What happened to you?" I asked.

"Honestly, I'm not even sure if I have the words to describe it, but when I saw how much pain you were in, I wanted to help. I reached out for you and was sucked into this world filled with clouds. I could hear voices but couldn't make out any sounds. The whole time, there was a searing pain in my chest that grew, extending into my arms and legs until finally a voice began speaking to me." Finn nodded to the tree. "It was her. She told me I'd taken on the darkness that had been killing her. It was the same as what I'd taken from Ivy, but stronger and unlike anything I've ever sensed before."

Neva huffed. "Yeah, tell me about it. I had to get it out of you."

Finn turned to her, resting his palms on Neva's shoulders. "Thank you. With your help and the mother tree, all of the dark magic within me is gone. I haven't felt this free in months."

That must have been why I noticed something different about him. I then wondered if that would change the way he thought of me but brushed the thoughts aside. What Finn and I had couldn't be easily dismissed.

Finn came back to my side and took my hand. "What now?" he asked.

"Should we go back to Mosi's? You both just exerted a lot of power trying to heal," Neva suggested.

My head shook. "I'm pretty sure we're both fine."

"The mother tree wouldn't have let any harm come to you," Ash said proudly.

"You can do more than speak to the trees, can't you?" I asked him, remembering how he'd sent the dark magic flying.

Ash blushed. "I can."

I nudged Finn. "You guys might have thought I was unique, but I'm pretty sure he's the only of his kind."

"What do you mean?" Finn asked.

I met Ash's eyes, and he nodded. "Ash here is a nature fae. The only one in existence if I have my history correct."

"Yes, I was born from the magic of the earth. I owe it my life, and I will guard it for as long as it needs me," Ash said.

I couldn't recall what happened to the last one, but I remembered reading a book as a child that told a fantasy tale about their kind and how only one ever lived at a time.

"We should go find Maeve now. She's on one of the tourist islands. Unless you need any other help," I said more to Ash than anyone else as I glanced around at the other trees and couldn't see any differences.

Ash shook his head. "The mother tree and I can take it from here. If it helps, the witch you seek is somewhere I can feel your energy at. Have you already searched the tourist islands before coming here?"

I met Finn's gaze. "She must be where we saw the alpha shifter Roman. Maybe that's why the sea witch dropped us there."

Finn's grip tightened on mine. "Thanks for the information. We need to get going."

That, he wasn't wrong about. Maia had told me Maeve was taking life that didn't belong to her.

Hopefully the wolf had escaped before the psycho's arrival.

"Now that the mother tree is safe, I can leave the island. Would you like my help?" Ash offered.

My head shook. "I don't think so. While you're powerful in your own way, you're not combat trained and still a child. You might look nearly twenty, but what are you? Eight or nine years old?"

He blushed again. "I am eight."

"Yeah, that's what I thought. You stay here and protect the trees like you've been doing. It's also important to the islands," I said.

Ash nodded, and I took Finn's hand, glancing up at him. "Ready to take on a fae-witch?" I asked.

"As we'll ever be," he replied, then reached back to grab Neva before teleporting all three of us out of there.

As we landed on the island, waves crashed against the beach, angry and ominous. "Well, Maeve's clearly been up to no good," I said.

"Why is she doing this?" Neva asked.

Even though I sensed the question was rhetorical, I felt compelled to answer. "She's a damned psychopath, and dark magic has a way of becoming addictive." Power rolled off my hands and toward the tree line. "She's here, and I sense death. Lots of it."

Finn stepped closer to me. "Please, don't do anything irrational."

I grinned. "We're going to be fine, Finnigan. It's just one fae hybrid. She's nothing."

"But Mosi said—"

"Mosi says a lot of things. We're going to be fine," I repeated, riding the high I still felt from the mother tree. Nothing was going to get me down.

A blast of power slammed into us, separating me

from Finn and Neva. I landed with half my body in the turbulent waves, and they'd been thrown toward the trees.

Maybe I spoke too soon.

My skin burned from the dark magic, but I wanted nothing to do with it. I drew on my own power, sparks flickering off me as the opposing magic collided. I fought against the tantalizing effects before pulling myself out of the water.

"What was that, Lucinda? I could have sworn you said I was *nothing*, but that can't be true," Maeve called from the tree line as she sauntered toward me in a one-piece black leather suit, crimson power twisting around her arms and hands.

"Oh, Margie. I certainly didn't stutter. You had to *steal* power. That makes you nothing in my book," I said, letting the warmth of my natural magic pull the water from my clothes and flow from my hands toward the sand.

Finn and Neva recovered from the initial blast and appeared at my side, but I hardly paid them any attention while I focused on what was happening within myself. Magic swirled at my core like normal, but there was an ethereal feeling to it. My skin warmed, my muscles felt stronger, and I stood taller. Whatever had happened between having the dark magic stripped from me and attaching myself to the mother tree, it had changed me fundamentally.

Where I was once hard edges and darkness, I was learning to become logical and calm. My thoughts were still the same—I had very few cares to give about the hybrid before me—but the difference was that I didn't look at her with anger at my center.

I was free from the hate I'd held on to for so long, and I was going to show Maeve that she might be powerful, but I was unrivaled. My power was something she'd yet to face, and it would be the last thing she saw before I removed her existence from this world.

Maeve bent to the sand, digging her fingers in, and waves of magic traveled through the beach, heading straight for us. I grabbed on to Neva as Finn and I used our wings to float just above the ground.

"While I had hoped for Zephyr to take care of you for me, I have no qualms about doing so myself. Taking your power will only fuel my own. You're not leaving this island," Maeve sneered, lowering her head to the ground as I sensed magic building within her again.

I laughed. "You keep telling yourself that, Mabel."

Her head snapped up, eyes crimson like a vampire and her previously silver hair turning black at the tips. "My name is Maeve Catherine Hastings, and you will show me some damn respect."

My eyes narrowed, meeting her twisted snarl. "Not today. Not ever."

I dropped Neva to the ground once it was clear and charged for Maeve, remembering Mosi's words not to underestimate her, but also feeling more powerful than I'd ever known. With my wings out and feathers hardened, I plucked several and threw them at Maeve as a distraction while I channeled my own energy.

She dodged each one, pulling a blade from behind her and thrusting it at me. I didn't pull my wing back and the dagger penetrated right through it, striking a nerve.

Shock rolled through me, both figuratively and literally. Nothing had ever cut through my feathers before. Sure, my wings had been battered and bruised, but never pierced.

Maeve laughed. "I'm going to break you before I kill you, and it's going to be the most rewarding moment of my life."

She was emotional about this fight, which didn't make any sense to me. I'd only met Maeve the one time before, but she knew who I was. That wasn't surprising to me at the time, but now I wondered if there was more to her hatred than just being a crazy bitch.

"You can certainly try, Molly." I landed behind her, grabbing her hair and yanking her head back as I drove one of my feathers through her chest.

She turned as I did so, punching me in the jaw with dark magic. My body recoiled as the hit lit my skin on fire, and I backed up several paces.

Neva was suddenly in the middle of me and Maeve, popping in and out of existence, moving around Maeve and keeping her distracted while Finn got closer.

Finn took my hand, our bond strengthening me as I readied for another attack, but before we could do anything together, heavy power settled over my mind.

After that, everything happened in slow motion as I took my first steps back toward the fight, trying to push Finn behind me as I registered what was happening.

Maeve flung her hands out and tilted her head back as a melody left her lips.

"Finn, go!" I screamed, but it was too late. She already had her claws into him.

Finn bowed before her while Neva and I moved in.

Maeve met my glare as she continued to call out with the siren's lure. Midnight-colored birds with holographic feathers and red eyes flew toward the beach under her control.

With Finn at her mercy, I hesitated on my next move, but Neva didn't. The elf threw her hands in the air and screamed like a banshee, forcing me to cover my ears and Maeve to stumble before she fell on her ass, but it was Finn I watched most.

He rolled to his side, blood dripping from his ears and a blade sticking out of his upper chest, dangerously close to his heart, and I had no idea how it had gotten there. No longer was there a calm within me. My body moved of its own accord, and Maeve was all I could see.

"This ends now," I snarled as I lunged for her, hands charged with power that wrapped around her neck.

As I yanked her toward me, she grinned. "Yes, I think it does."

When my fingers pressed into her skin with the intention of killing the fae-witch, Maeve slammed her head into mine. "Your elf might have broken through my siren's call, but that's not the only trick I have."

I squeezed harder, but Maeve wasn't deterred by my power one bit. Instinct told me to back away and regroup, but she wasn't having any of that.

Maeve grabbed hold of my wrists and twisted, bones cracking. "You took everything from me," she spat, her voice quivering in anger. "It should have been me at Zephyr's side, and instead he chose *you*."

Understanding poured into me. "I would have gladly let you take my place," I said, trying to reevaluate my situation. Neva was breathing heavily next to Finn on the ground, and I was on my own for the moment.

Maeve surprised me by letting go of my wrists, then clapped her hands. Power knocked me back and onto my ass at the tree line, even further from Neva and Finn.

A storm was brewing above the ocean waters. The sky darkened as the light diminished, and I knew we were running out of time. Leaning against the nearest tree, I pushed through the pain and stood. Maeve would not best me. She would not take anyone from me.

Maeve stalked toward me. "I should have killed you the moment you showed up at my house, but I thought, 'Why not test your strengths and let someone else do the dirty work my guards had failed to do?' As disappointed as I was that you survived a fight with a siren, I have to say I'm grateful now."

Even as I thought about what an idiot she was for having no clue the sirens were all dead, a peace filled me. I drew on my own power, but before I could act, voices echoed in my mind.

Heal and fight with your heart, Lucinda.

The tree's branches above me swayed as the wind blew harder around us. The essence of the mother tree filled me, and I was reminded of what I was capable of. Of who I was.

My head hung low as I pressed my palms against the rough palm tree bark, buying time.

"Giving up already? Such a disappointment, but I guess I shouldn't be surprised," Maeve snickered.

My eyes lifted just enough to meet her stare. "I'm really tired of people calling me that."

With renewed energy from the trees, I stalked toward her, thrusting my hands forward while teal and white magic poured from my body, wrapping around Maeve. She fought through it, and we collided in the middle with a loud bang.

Dark and light magic went to war as the rest of the world fell away. Hit after hit, neither of us gained the upper hand, but I wasn't weakening. I pressed on, trying to ignore the fact that Neva and Finn had been in a bad way the last time I'd had eyes on them.

Neva was powerful, and Finn had every reason to live. I chose to believe they'd be fine as I drew on the endless amount of magic at my disposal.

My wings cut into Maeve as her nails raked along my exposed skin, each of us drawing blood just as quickly as we healed. We were too evenly matched. As we moved along the beach exchanging blows, I did my best to keep her away from the water. With siren blood in her, I didn't know how it might affect her and I wasn't willing to find out.

"Your friends are dying. You should really do something about that," Maeve taunted, but I ignored the ache in my chest caused by her words.

If I allowed her to distract me, we would all be dead anyway.

The storm worsened around us, unlike anything I'd ever seen in the fae realm. When it rained here, it was only for the benefit of the crops and more tropical, but there was nothing beneficial about the darkening skies above.

Waves crashed closer, the beach growing smaller by the second until the water split. Maeve backed away from me, hands holding her head as blood dripped from her eyes.

"What are you doing to me?" she roared, but I had no idea why. *I* wasn't doing a damned thing.

I glanced between the water and Maeve, trying to decide if it was worth striking her while she was down or if I should see how things played out.

"Maeve, you took something that didn't belong to you and used it for evil intentions. You disrupted the balance of my waters," the sea queen Alana's voice sounded before her form shimmered into appearance within the turbulent waves.

She nodded at me, but it was the sight behind her that caught my attention. A man waded in the water, glaring at me just before he dove back under the waves, a silver tail flicking behind him as he disappeared.

Alana strolled onto the beach wearing the same sleek black gown as before, hands at her sides, and called me to her. "You made this mess. You need to clean it up."

"Yeah, because I've just been playing with her this whole time for fun," I droned before glancing behind me, searching for the others.

Finn was positioned against a tree with his eyes closed as Neva fought against the creatures I'd seen earlier. I moved to go to them, but Alana grasped my arm.

"Your mate lives. Finish this before you make me angry," she said, eyeing the withering Maeve at our feet.

My eyes shifted toward the sky above. "You're not already angry?"

She smirked at me. "I've only shown you my good side, Lucinda. You wouldn't survive being in my presence if I was truly upset. As of now, I'm just annoyed."

After all I'd seen, I was going to take Alana's word for it. With Maeve and Zephyr, I had enough to deal with. I didn't need to make another enemy by being stubborn.

Maeve broke through whatever Alana had done to her and launched herself at me again, but I was ready for her. I brought my wing in front of me and slashed across her chest. Maeve let out a bellow as blood dripped from the wound and floated through the air toward Alana.

"I won't let you take this from me like everything else." Maeve's voice thundered over the still-brewing storm, crimson magic swirling around her.

"That's where you're wrong. I never took anything from you before today, but I will gladly take your life now." I goaded her with a grin and slashed at her again with my sharp feathers.

Her own emotions were going to be her downfall. She hated me too much to win. I understood then why she never fought me before, why she'd sent me into the depths of the ocean hoping I'd become victim to the sea creatures she would never have been able to beat.

Maeve knew she was nothing on her own, but she was too damned stubborn to allow people into her life that would elevate her. It was a mistake I had almost made myself, and I realized then how much alike we really were.

"I feel sorry for you, Maeve. I hope you find peace in the next life," I said, using her correct name for the first time to her face as I struck her with both of my wings and unleashed my full power at the same time.

Her aqua eyes widened as her arms flung back from the blast and my feathers cut into her stomach then across her neck. She floundered for a moment as the life in her eyes faded. She fell to the ground, blood no longer floating toward Alana, but instead, seeping into the sands.

"You've changed since we last met, Lucinda," the

sea queen murmured as she tucked the vial of blood into the top of her sleek dress.

Instead of responding to her, I turned and ran for Neva and Finn. More than a dozen birds, monkeys, and a few smaller animals I didn't look too closely at lay lifeless and contorted in the bloodied dirt. Neva rocked back and forth next to Finn with her arms wrapped around her knees.

Finn was awake, moving slowly, and nodded for me to tend to Neva first. I pressed a hand to her back, and she flinched, peeking up at me with tears in her eyes.

"They wouldn't stop. I didn't want to kill them," she cried.

"What do you mean?" They were just animals. I didn't understand what she was so upset about.

Neva shuddered and hiccupped. "The fae we'd seen at Maeve's previous house… She turned them all into those creatures. I had to take their lives before they took ours, but they didn't know what they were doing. It wasn't fair."

"If I could bring them all back and kill them myself, I would," I said softly, knowing if they'd chosen to stay with that batshit-crazy hybrid, then they damn well knew what they were doing. Maybe not in the moment, but they knew what was coming: death.

A thought occurred to me. Maybe I *could* bring the animals back and take those deaths from Neva. I leaned over, reaching toward the nearest bird with singe marks on its wings and dangling head. My hand pressed forcefully down onto the creature softly once, then harder each time I repeated the action.

Nothing happened.

Frustration filled me as Neva's crying quieted. I wanted to do this for her. I would do this for her. Except I didn't know how to force this part of my magic to work. I moved on to a monkey after I'd nearly broken every bone in the bird. I touched each of the animals, but nothing worked.

Finn joined me with the color back in his face, but more blood than I was comfortable with stained his shirt.

Before I could ask if he was okay, Alana stood over us. "You can't bring them back, Lucinda. It was their time. These fae chose power over integrity, and this is their price to pay."

"But it shouldn't be *hers*." I nodded toward Neva, who had stopped rocking but clearly wasn't okay as her vacant eyes stared out into the ocean.

"No, and she will have to work through her demons to find acceptance. Neva did nothing wrong today, and as much as you want, you can't convince her of something she has to process on her own, just like you seem to have done," Alana replied as the clouds cleared above and the water began to calm again.

"You'll need to go. The power exchanged here won't go unnoticed by the king, and he will come with an army," she added.

"Let him," I challenged.

"Now is not the time or place. You will go to the

castle as planned, but you need your own army, Lucinda. Don't lose sight of what is right when you're so close to the finish," Alana said.

I grunted. "Have you been speaking to Mosi?"

She grinned. "Mosi is a smart fae. You made the right choice to trust him."

A splash in the water caught my attention, and the silver tail thrashed around from the mermaid, or was it merman? Either way, he was out there and clearly impatient.

I nodded behind her. "Your guard dog seems ready to leave."

Alana turned back toward the ocean, her hands glowing gold and bringing the water closer to us. Before the waves could get near enough to touch, I was standing with Finn at my side and in front of Neva who hadn't moved much.

"Is that a mermaid?" Finn asked, rubbing his chest that no longer seemed injured.

The fish-man snarled, showcasing sharp teeth that snapped at us.

"Enough, Edgar," Alana reprimanded.

Uncontrollable laughter left me as I took in the sea creature wading in the shallow surf before us.

The sea queen glared at me next. "That's really not necessary." Her power washed over me, and I silenced my amusement.

"Nice to see you, Edgar," Finn said, grabbing hold of my hand.

Edgar didn't reply as his clawed hands flexed at his side.

"So, is he out on good behavior?" I asked.

Alana stroked Edgar's cheek. "I can never go too long without my mate. As mad as I was at him, this works out better for us. He is of the ocean now, and we will never be apart."

Edgar met her stare, his unfamiliar eyes softening toward the witch. His mouth opened and closed, but no words came out.

"I know, my love. We'll go home in a moment," she replied, then turned back to us. "Edgar can't leave the water, and he can only speak to me until his hatred for the fae is gone. I want to remind you that I gave you the siren blood on the condition you would not hurt my mate even when I knew it would be used for dark magic."

There was a threat in her words that none of us missed.

"You have nothing to fear from us as long as you keep the leash on him nice and tight," I replied, and he snapped his teeth at me again. "I bite back," I said with a smirk to Edgar.

Alana waved a hand and the water receded, taking Edgar with it. "You don't need to antagonize him. He's paying for the things he's done."

I waggled my brows. "Oh, I bet he is."

She ignored my comment, nodding toward the bloodied beach. "Leave now, and I'll clean the rest of this up. The guards are on their way."

My hesitation must have been clear, because Finn grabbed Neva, then reached for me again. "Thank you, Alana. We are happy to repay you for your help today if you ever need it."

She nodded. "Here's to hoping that is never the case."

CHAPTER 10

*E*verything within me ached now that the adrenaline had worn off. My magic had soothed the worst of my wounds, but the gouge to my wing hadn't healed, and the bone-deep ache in my muscles was nearly as bad as it had been when I'd almost died at the castle.

After we appeared on Mosi's island, my steps faltered, and Finn hooked his arm under my own. "What's wrong, Lucinda?"

"I'm just… tired," I replied as Neva disappeared and reappeared within the same second.

She shoved a bottle of clear liquid at me. "Drink this."

My hands wouldn't cooperate, so she opened it up and Finn took the bottle, tilting it up to my lips. The liquid was cool and tingling against my tongue as soon as it hit. I eagerly gulped down as much as Finn gave me.

"What is this?" Finn asked as renewed energy filtered through my limbs.

"Something to combat the dark energy from Maeve. Lucinda's not affected like before, but it's clinging to her. I can see it all around her exposed skin," Neva replied, and I shoved Finn away before any of it could get on him.

"Well, how the hell do I get it off?" I bit out, already feeling like myself again.

"I don't know," she answered with a frown.

Then, I remembered Finn's injury. "How are you okay already? Fae healing doesn't normally work *that* fast."

He shrugged. "Alana."

Well, that was nice of her to help my mate and not offer the same to me. Just as I considered going to find Yury in hopes he was still hanging around and done with my sword, cold arms wrapped around me from behind.

"You're back." Olida sighed.

"I told you she would be fine," Mosi huffed, walking up as I turned around.

Olida let go of me and whirled around to stab her finger into Mosi's chest. "You also said she might die, so forgive me if I needed to see for myself."

Finn's chest rumbled as he stepped closer to me. "Excuse me?"

Mosi glared at Olida. "Nothing. Like I've said before, the future is never set in stone. Your trip to the trees changed the course I had foreseen."

"And what course was that?" Finn asked, vibrating with rage next to me.

Mosi sighed. "Does it really matter now? Everyone is back and fine."

It was my turn to be irritated. "Just because we're standing doesn't mean we're fine, Mosi." I knew Neva wasn't okay, and if Mosi knew something that could have prevented what happened to her, then we were going to have words. Lots of them.

"How many times do I have to explain to you that my ability might predict the future, but it isn't all-knowing?"

Oddly enough, that made sense.

"Okay, have it your way for now, but what happens next?" I asked.

Mosi stepped closer to me, and Finn's hold tightened. "Easy, Finn. I'm checking her injuries," Mosi said softly, raising his hands.

Finn nodded, trusting the fae and backing away just a step. Mosi didn't need to check on me, though. After drinking whatever Neva had given me, I felt better. The aches and pains were gone, and I was ready to storm the castle. Maeve had been dealt with, and dusk was coming soon. It was all working out perfectly.

"We need to get you into the healing tank," Mosi said after just one touch on my shoulder. "It will strip the dark magic clinging to you. If you hadn't merged with the mother tree, Maeve's power would have turned you or killed you if you weren't strong enough to fight being turned."

My brow furrowed. "What do you mean 'merged with the mother tree'? I healed her, but I didn't become a damn tree, and Neva's drink is already helping with the dark magic."

Mosi and Olida shared a look. One I didn't care for.

"What? What else haven't you told me?" I sighed, growing too tired by the second to be angry. Maybe whatever Neva gave me wasn't working all that well.

Olida stepped forward, looping her arm through mine. "I think this conversation needs to be had over drinks and food. I promise, it's the last of its kind."

I turned to Neva and Finn. "We do this and then head to the castle?"

Neva shook her head. "You two go with them. I need some time. I'll be in my pocket realm. Call for me when you're ready to leave again."

Without waiting for a reply from any of us, Neva disappeared, taking a bit of my heart with her.

Neva had given a lot for me over the years, and as much as I wanted to keep her around now, I wasn't going to call for her later. She didn't need to see any more death, not after seeing how it affected her on that island. It was too much to ask. Even I wasn't that selfish. We could finish Zephyr without Neva.

Finn stepped closer, pulling me away from Olida, and his hands rubbed my arms. "She's going to be okay."

"I know, but I didn't want this for her. I didn't want her to have to take a life, let alone a dozen of them. She told me things about her past, told me why she didn't like to use her magic."

His fingers tightened around my hands. "Not everything is your responsibility, Lucy. Neva knew what she was doing when she chose to come with us."

He was right, but knowing that didn't make the situation any better. It was still shit all around.

Olida went to Mosi. "Let's go back to our place. Then, I promise. Final preparations for going to the castle will be made," she said before they both disappeared.

I hesitated to follow them. "No matter what they say, we can't wait much longer, Finn. You saw South Island. The others are probably just the same, and there might never be a perfect moment to go back to the castle. At some point, we're just going to have to see what happens. Plus, the more destruction I see, the more I really want to burn Zephyr's castle down."

He grinned at me. "I never thought I'd say it, but I really enjoy that side of you. Just remember, we still need someone to rule the fae realm, or other supernaturals will come here thinking they can take the place over. Whoever rules next might want somewhere to live while doing so."

I waved my hand in the air. "They can build a new castle. Probably better anyway. The demons in that castle are deep within its bones."

Though it had never come up, I sort of assumed Mosi and Olida would take over and they could rule from this island anyway. Sure, changes would need to be made, but they didn't take me as the types to need a monstrosity like the current castle in order to rule.

"We'll figure it out soon enough. Let's go see what Mosi and Olida have to say, so we can end this nightmare," Finn said and held his hand out.

I placed mine in his as he teleported us back to the hut. When we arrived, Mosi and Olida were waiting outside.

"We're going to take this meeting to the healing tank, actually. Neva's fix is temporary, and the dark magic from the siren's blood will only continue to drain you if we don't get it off," Mosi said, gesturing toward the trees behind their house.

I had already assumed that and gladly followed them with Finn at my side. My movements were becoming sluggish again, and it hadn't even been ten minutes since Neva left us. Even after only a day without it, the heaviness of the dark magic wasn't something I ever wanted to go back to.

I may have thought I'd been calling the shots since I'd left the fae realm, but I knew better now. I'd been weak to the voice, and that would never happen again.

We arrived at what looked like a hot spring made inside a huge rock. A small hot-tub-sized pool of water sat between a handful of trees with steam rising from the flat surface and water clear enough to see the bottom of. Carved inside the boulder were two seats, and it was maybe four or five feet deep.

My skin tingled as we stood over it. "So, I just get in?"

"Yes. You'll want to submerge yourself to the bottom for at least a minute, then you should be fine to just sit on one of the seats for the next little while," Olida answered.

My fingers went to my shirt, and Finn stepped in front of me. "What do you think you're doing?" he grumbled, holding my hands.

"Uh, getting in the water." I tugged harder on my shirt, but he wasn't letting up.

"Leave them," he growled.

"Leave what? My clothes? I don't think so. I'm not ashamed of my body, and it's not like Mosi is single and looking to mingle. Calm down." I stepped back, ready to use magic to get naked, but Olida moved in.

"You're newly bonded, Lucinda. Be nice to your other half. Even when he acts like a caveman." She smirked, and a breeze blew over me.

When I looked down, I was no longer in the jeans and shirt I'd been in before, but I was wearing a white cotton dress, much like the one I'd had on when I'd woken up on the beach my first day here.

Memories of that afternoon filtered through as I met Finn's heated gaze. I knew without having to ask that he was thinking of the sex we'd had that changed both of our lives.

Olida practically shoved me toward the water. "You're wasting time with hormones. You'll have the opportunity for that later."

Finn blushed, but I just grinned back at her. I had no shame in my game.

As I stepped over the edge of the rock and my toes dipped into the heated water first, my muscles seized, and Olida ended up pushing me all the way in. I heard Finn's objections just as my head went under the water.

My brain was telling my arms to move so that I could come back up and reassure him I was okay, but nothing would respond to my commands. My body was locked down, and I sank lower into the water that was not nearly as shallow as it had appeared when I glanced in from above.

When I finally hit the bottom, everything around me was dark. There wasn't even a glimmer of light. My skin burned and cooled in rapid succession until I was ready to rip myself to shreds from the conflicting feelings. Except I couldn't make any of my limbs work on my own.

I was starting to panic that I was stuck down there when my arms and legs started to thrash around, smashing into the rock and bruising me up even more. My head hit the stone, causing my vision to tunnel and my body to go limp.

I fought to stay conscious as the light above me grew bigger. Hands grabbed at me, and I sucked in a breath as my head broke the surface.

Finn's warm hand pounded on my back until I choked up what felt like a gallon of water. "You're okay, Lucinda. I have you."

Once my coughing fit was over, I relaxed back into the water, shrugging off Finn's hold. "Well, that was fun." My shoulders rolled back, everything already feeling heaps better, including my head.

Mosi rubbed his jaw. "I can't say I agree, but at least it's done."

I got comfortable on one of the stone seats, and Finn settled in behind me with only his arms in the water.

"So, what's this last bit of doom and gloom that the two of you have been hiding?" I asked.

Olida tsked. "Not hiding. We only just found out when Mosi contacted one of the other feathered fae. Technically, you haven't been around for us to tell you, so you can't be mad this time."

My arms and legs pushed through the water as it rushed between my fingers and toes. "Right. Well, spill it."

Mosi began, "We will want the feathered fae with us when we attack the castle—"

I cut him off. "'We' as in you're coming with us, finally?"

He nodded. "It's time for my part in all of this. Olida will stay here with those who don't wish to fight and the children of the island. I will lead the rest of them to battle against the fae who have been forced to protect the walls that coward hides behind."

Mosi's hands wrapped around the edge of the healing waters until his knuckles turned white.

"What sort of bone do you have to pick with Zephyr?" I asked before he could continue again.

Olida wrapped her fingers around Mosi's. "It's not just Zephyr. It's all the leaders like him that we fight against. No fae should be treated like you and so many others have."

"Did the two of you know Maeve was being groomed to be Zephyr's pet before he found me?" I raised a brow, watching their faces for any sign of recognition.

Mosi shook his head. "I didn't, but it makes sense now, given all we've learned. She was very reckless with her decisions."

I couldn't have agreed more. "Okay, now that we cleared that up. What did you learn about me from the feathered fae dude you called?"

Mosi and Olida shared one of their looks I hated. One that told me whatever they learned was worse than anything they might have told us before.

"You can heal people on the brink of death. You've saved those closest to you and you will continue to try to save more people as time goes on, but you can't," Olida finally said.

"Why not?" I asked her. If I was supposed to be this new me who thought of others before myself, how was I supposed to stand by idly if I saw someone dying?

"Because you'll kill yourself in the process otherwise."

CHAPTER 11

I blinked repeatedly at Olida until she laughed, then I found my composure and glared at her. "What's so funny?"

"I've never seen you speechless before. I think I might write this moment down on the calendar."

My hands twitched under the water, but I kept a handle on my actions, choosing to think first.

Olida started to speak again, but Mosi placed a hand on her shoulder. "For once, love, I think it might be better if I explain this."

She glanced between me and Finn as he vibrated behind me. "I think you might be right."

"So, what does she mean exactly?" Finn asked, leaning on the edge of the rocks as I turned to sit on my knees, still in the water, so I could see all of their faces.

"We learned that Lucinda gives a piece of her soul away every time she saves a life. Even if that life was never meant to be taken, there has to be a trade with this kind of magic. It was minuscule when she saved you and your sister, but with Maddox, it was more significant and the mother tree? Well, that could have killed her then if you hadn't interfered."

Fucking hell.

I knew there was a reason I'd never been a good person before. Good deeds never went unpunished.

"Are you saying my soul resides in Finn, Ivy, Maddox, and the mother tree?" I asked.

Finn growled next to me. Probably not a great idea for him to visualize any part of me being inside of his soon-to-be brother-in-law.

"Yes and no. A part of your soul was used to keep them on this side of the supernatural veil, but it's only your essence that is left within the others. Well, all except the mother tree. She does own part of your soul now," Mosi answered.

He said the words so casually, as if they weren't a big freaking deal. "What does that mean? Can she control me?"

I hadn't sensed any maliciousness from Maia when I'd been connected to her, but people weren't born evil, either. With this new information, my guard would be up.

Mosi shook his head. "Not in the way you fear, Lucinda. You can speak to her through the trees, and she can provide you strength the same way, but she cannot influence your decisions."

I remembered leaning against the tree when we'd fought Maeve and feeling better after using the trunk to help me back up. Interesting. I hadn't thought much of it then. Either way, I still wasn't overly fond of having my soul ripped away little by little.

"How many times can I save people before I kick the bucket?" I asked, and Finn flinched next to me.

Olida shook her head at my crassness while Mosi answered. "That can't be answered, unfortunately. It depends on the severity of the situation. You wouldn't be able to save another entity like the mother tree, but you might be able to help others another few dozen times if they're comparable to Ivy and Finn."

Fae lived centuries. I didn't like knowing I had the power to bring someone back but that I maybe only had thirty times left that I could use it. And that was only if I was picky about who lived and died. Not that I planned to spend a lot of time around people that were dying, but still. My stomach twisted.

"I don't like this ability," I said.

Finn held me closer. "Neither do I, but we'll work it out."

"Just don't change who you are, Lucy, and everything will be just fine," Olida said, handing me a steaming cup of hot toddy from a stump behind her. Something I wished I'd had before they'd dropped that bomb on me.

I downed the warm drink in a few gulps. "I'll take three more of those, please."

Olida nodded and poured another that I gladly took.

"What now? You mentioned the other feathered fae coming to help. Are they already here, and can we head to the castle once Lucy is done in here?" Finn asked, reminding me I shouldn't get drunk on whiskey and self-pity if I was planning to kill a king later that night.

"Victor is on his way with the others. Don't expect to get to know many of them. They're reclusive and prefer to remain unseen. Victor will likely be the only one you formally meet. He's been my friend for over a century," Mosi answered.

"When do we leave for the castle?" I asked, holding the third refill close to my lips.

Mosi sighed. "I know you're eager to get there, but I'd prefer we wait until tomorrow night. It will give us time to coordinate with the feathered fae and perfect our attack. As far as I can tell, nothing should change if we wait."

He expected an objection from me, but I was damned tired after the day I'd had. Saving a mother tree and killing a psycho fae-witch-sort-of-siren supernatural weren't the easiest things I'd done. I downed the third glass without guilt.

"Tomorrow it is, but I'm done talking for now if that's all you have to share." I turned to Olida and she handed me the pot of alcohol. "Thank you."

She winked. "Put it to good use."

I smirked back and grabbed Finn's hand as I got out of the water. My plans for the next several hours included drinking the rest of the spiced drink and convincing Finn with my body that everything was going to be fine. I needed the distraction, and we needed the bonding time.

Except, I thought of one other thing and halted my steps. "What about the sword? Is Yury still here, and did he finish it?"

Mosi smiled, wrinkles forming at the sides of his eyes. "Yes, he finished and believes your idea is genius. He made a couple slight changes, but overall, it's exactly as you envisioned."

As curious as I was to know these changes, they could wait a bit longer given we weren't leaving until the following evening.

"Good. Glad the not-witch can listen on occasion. We'll be back to meet the feathered fae later." I tugged on Finn's arm and teleported back to our hut with the hot toddy pot in hand.

Finn lifted me up into his arms and cradled me close as soon as we reappeared, even though I was still wet from the water. "Thank you for this," he said.

I shrugged and backed up a step to dry myself off with magic. "We both needed it. I'm not stubborn enough to deny that."

He tightened his hold on me with one arm when I was done and used the other to open the door before kicking it closed, taking the pot from me, then tossing me on the bed. His sexy lips lifted into a smile as he headed for the cups, grabbing two.

The cotton dress I'd been changed into at the healing waters was too pure for the thoughts running through my mind, so I used magic to change my clothes. When Finn's back was to me, I watched as the white cotton turned into black silk with a bra top that made my boobs look better than ever. The silky material flowed down in soft waves, ending just at my ass. I moved to my side, flicking my hair back and resting my chin on one hand while I watched Finn pour a drink for each of us.

My eyes stayed on the back of his head, so I could see his reaction as soon as he turned around. Since the moment I met Finn, I'd often wondered how he truly saw me. Sure, I knew there was attraction and that he cared about me, but there was something deeper I was looking for, something more. I just didn't know what it was until the moment his stare landed on me.

The silver turned to charcoal within an instant as his eyes widened. His lips opened slightly, as if he was speechless, and his hold on the cups faltered, but not enough to drop the mugs I no longer had any interest in.

Finn took a hesitant step toward me, unseen magic pouring off him and heating the room. My finger curved, summoning him to me. He set the drinks down, still seeming unsure of his movements.

"Finnigan, don't you dare be scared of me now," I purred, lowering my eyes at him, a stray piece of hair falling onto my face.

Within a blink, gone was the uncertain fae, and in his place was the alpha male I'd only seen glimpses of thus far. He stalked toward me, shedding his clothes piece by piece until he was at the edge of the bed, left only in tight boxer briefs.

My head tilted up, and my lips curved as his hand

reached out, fingers grasping my chin as Finn lowered himself until we were eye level.

"You're more than I ever wished for." His words sent heat straight to my core.

I tilted my head back. "And all yours."

Finn's touch moved from my chin and down my exposed neck and arms until he reached the edge of the silk. His fingers fisted around the fabric. "As much as I like this, it's going to have to go, Lucinda."

I trailed a nail over the bulge between his hips. "If mine goes, so does yours."

"Not yet." He grunted, then shoved me back onto the bed.

My hair fanned out behind me, and I lifted my arms above my head, digging my fingers into the soft pillow. "Well, then. What first?"

Instead of answering with words, Finn lowered himself to the bed, kneeling over me. "I'm going to love you."

Before I could contest his use of love, his head dropped down, and he lifted the silk, burying his face between my legs. All objections forgotten, I let my knees fall to the sides as one of his hands trailed up to caress my chest and the other joined his tongue. I moaned louder with every flick of his tongue.

No longer could I leave my hands behind my head. Instead, I sank one of them into Finn's hair, holding him right where I needed him most while my other hand joined his on my chest. My back arched as the orgasm built with every lick and thrust.

Finn's fingers twisted and pressed against my most sensitive parts, sending me over the edge. I let out a guttural scream as my nails dug into his head and palm. "Holy Gods, why have you never done that before?"

His head tilted up, eyes shining with mischief. "I couldn't play all of my cards right away."

I yanked him up, drawing him toward me. "Finn Barlow, you better reveal all of your cards right now."

He held himself up on his elbows, fingers brushing my hair back before his thumb traced over my lips. "You don't want that."

There was a challenge in his voice. One I wouldn't back down from. "I believe otherwise." My hand reached around his backside, squeezing his ass.

Finn raised a brow, the charcoal in his eyes lessening back to the soft silver. "Lucinda Morrow." He paused, moving closer until his lips were only an inch from mine. "I love you."

Now was my turn to hesitate, except I didn't. I felt his words in my heart, at the very core of my being. I had no doubts he meant them, and while I would have thought they'd scare the shit out of me, a sense of peace settled over me.

"I know you do." I gripped the sides of his face, kissing him fiercely, tasting myself on his tongue as we continued to ravage each other. I didn't know if I would ever be able to return his words, but I wasn't afraid of Finn's feelings, and that was more than I ever thought possible before meeting him.

Without missing a beat, he kissed me deeply, and both of us were free of all clothing as Finn slid into me. At first, his movements were slow and precise, striking deep and holding tight. As I met his thrusts with those of my own, he picked up speed.

I threw my head back as a second orgasm ran through me, but Finn wasn't done. He slowed only until I came down from my high, then grinned. "Ready for more?"

"I'm always ready for more when it comes to you," I replied, leaning up to kiss him again.

When I tried to pull away, Finn followed my movements, keeping me close. I opened my eyes to find him already watching me as he continued to kiss and build me up all over again. This time he kept with the slow movements, continually watching my eyes.

"I like you," I whispered to him softly.

He smiled, repeating my earlier words. "I know you do."

Finn thrusted faster, each stroke reaching deeper inside me. The veins in his neck strained as I reached my climax and clenched around him tightly. He closed his eyes, pushing into me hard as he found his release. Breathless, he collapsed onto me, our sweaty bodies pressed together once more, and he buried his face in my hair.

"Promise me something?" he asked, turning his head so we were nose-to-nose.

"What's that?"

"You won't do anything reckless tomorrow. I know

we all want this to be over, but not at the expense of lives if we can help it. Especially not yours. I've only just found you. I won't lose you again. We'll come at Zephyr as many times as it takes, but only when it poses minimal risk."

His fingers traced over the curves of my chest, and I grabbed his hand. "We've given him too much time, Finn. There won't ever be a moment when the risk is slight. We're going to be walking into a war tomorrow, and not everyone will be coming home. You have to understand that now or you won't survive the fight."

I said the words almost as much for him as I did for me, and I wanted Finn prepared for what he might see. I didn't need him distracted by the sight of dead bodies, possibly the bodies of people we cared about. He needed to turn off his emotions for a short time, or he was only going to be a liability in the battle against Zephyr's guards.

"I can't accept that," he said.

"Then, you can't come. I have no problem asking Yury to spell this hut and keep you trapped until we're done. People die in my world, Finn. If you want to be part of it, you need to accept the risks that one day it might be me. I won't be kept in a bubble or asked to be someone I'm not. I'm a warrior. I always have been, and always will be."

Finn nodded. "I know. I'm sorry. I just had to try."

I tapped him on the nose, not at all offended he'd attempted to sway me. "It's cute when you try."

The grin that followed broke our tense moment, and

I breathed a little easier. Sure, I was nervous about what to expect at the castle, but I wasn't afraid—not of Zephyr or of dying.

One way or another, this ended with blood and it ended within the next two days.

CHAPTER 12

*L*ater, just before the sun had set, Finn and I left the hut. I'd been worried about Neva and curious to meet the other fae like me. Something told me they weren't going to be anything like me or Mosi. While I didn't think I was similar to Mosi in most ways, we at least didn't hide out from the world.

The others were probably more like Yury and that was going to be entertaining. At least, I hoped so.

When we arrived back at Mosi and Olida's, I was tackle-hugged from behind. "Hello, Ivy," I droned without even having to see her.

"Olida told me if I bothered the two of you, she'd make me do the dishes after tonight's feast. I hate dishes." She pouted as Finn and I turned toward her and Maddox.

"We heard about the tree and Maeve. I'm sorry I wasn't there to help," Maddox said.

Finn clasped his hand on Maddox's shoulder. "It's okay. You were right where you belonged."

Maddox nodded, but I could see he wasn't quite alright with everything. Ivy watched him closely as well, a frown on her face.

I nudged her. "Have you had Olida's *special* drink yet?"

She glared at me. "I don't think so. The last time I drank with you, I forgot hours of my life."

"If I block out the breakdown you had, it was quite amusing if I do say so," I replied.

Finn squeezed my hand. "Be careful with my sister. I need to talk with Maddox."

I gave him an eyeroll and sighed, waving a hand for him to go. If Ivy insisted on hanging out with me, then it was up to her to be careful.

The guys disappeared, and Ivy grinned at me, a light in her eyes that I hadn't seen since my earlier days on their farm.

"Aren't you supposed to be going through emotional turmoil? Why are you so happy?" I asked, because it was too weird to me that she was this okay after being tortured within the castle. Or maybe I was slightly jealous, considering it had taken me years to move past.

She looped her arm through mine, pulling me away from the hut I'd been headed to. I tried to object, but the fae was stronger than I'd given her credit for.

"Mosi and Olida are busy and asked not to be

interrupted. You missed your chance to be included in the meeting when you stayed shacked up with my brother." She shuddered. "While I'm not sure why, I'm glad. I've never seen him happier."

I knew enough about Finn. I wasn't concerned with what she thought about us or him; I wanted to know what was going on with her. "And you? What is happening with all this?" I pointed to her face, hoping she understood and would finally answer my questions.

Ivy's hold on me tightened as we entered the trees. "Olida. She's quite the healer. Nothing like me, but incredible all the same."

I recalled a memory of one of my first conversations with Olida. She'd told me how her abilities worked differently for each person, but I'd never wanted her to take my pain away. It was what made me who I was, or who I thought I wanted to be then.

Though, as I stared at Ivy, I knew her joy was what made her who she was, and I understood where she was going with her words.

"Olida took your pain away," I said.

Ivy nodded. "I still remember being there and the things they did to me, but it's more like watching a movie that I don't believe is real. I know it is, but I don't let the memories affect me. I'm choosing to be happy. I wasn't going to let that asshole keep me from living my life any longer. He'd already stolen too much of my time."

Her logic made sense, but it wasn't something I could have ever done for myself. Olida had been right. My pain had made me who I was, and while I hadn't been good at thinking before acting, I knew now I wasn't the monster I tried to be—who Zephyr tried to turn me into.

"Well, good for you, but if you're so okay, then what slithered into Maddox's ass and died?" I asked.

Ivy snorted. "You certainly have a way with words, Lucy." She continued leading us through the trees, making our way to the beach. She didn't answer my question, and I wasn't going to force her to. The silence was welcoming for me.

When we arrived at the water's edge, the sun was almost finished setting, casting orange, red, and yellow rays across the water's ever-moving surface. I think that was why I'd always been drawn to the ocean. Nothing stopped it. The waves always came, moving through whatever was in its path. While I liked to pretend that was me, I knew it wasn't the case.

I'd have come for Zephyr long ago if it was.

We came to the spot I always liked to sit, and I unhooked Ivy's arm from mine and settled onto the log. Ivy followed my lead, still remaining silent until the moon crested, and the sky darkened.

"Maddox is a great man. I've loved him since the moment I met him. He is funny, kind, smart, and handsome. He is everything except the one thing he believes he needs to be." Ivy sighed heavily, and I filled in the blank.

"He's not your mate."

She shook her head. "It was never a problem before. We knew what we were giving up—the kind of love you and Finn have—but ours felt just as epic. When I thought I was going to die anyway, not being true mates became even less important."

I wanted to correct her that Finn and I didn't have a great love story. We were mates and had great sex, sure... but love story, we were not. Except she continued on, so I let it go.

"While you guys were gone, we spent a lot of time with Olida and Mosi. They talked about the two of you, and we watched them. Their bond is tangible. You can see it in the way they look at each other, even in the way they speak. Maddox is nothing if not romantic, and he wants that for me."

My brow furrowed. "Why would he do that to himself? He fought like hell to get you back. I had to talk him off the edge a couple of times. I won't do it again if it's of his own doing."

Ivy grinned, patting my knee. "Because he loves me."

"That makes absolutely no sense to me," I replied.

"It will one day, when you're ready. For now, I've done my best to convince him that I want no one else. I have my epic love. Even if it's not the one I was destined for, Maddox is all I want."

"So, you're really okay, and Maddox is just being a stubborn man? No other world-ending problem we need to worry about?" I asked, hoping to change the subject from romance.

"Well, I wouldn't say Zephyr's existence is world-ending, but he's still a problem," Olida's voice sounded from behind us.

"Hey, crazy old lady. Quit eavesdropping on people. It's rude," I said with a smirk as I peeked over my shoulder at her.

Olida shrugged. "It's what makes me endearing to you, and it keeps my life interesting, so I don't think I'll be stopping anytime soon."

Ivy stood, taking me with her. "The meeting is over?"

"Yes. Victor would like to meet Lucinda. Finn and Maddox are already there. They tried to come get you, but I insisted they let me," she replied.

"Insisted or threatened?" I teased.

"Po-tay-to, po-tah-to. Come on, let's go. You have to meet Victor, then we'll go see Yury and get the sword. You'll want to practice with it tomorrow before we leave," Olida said.

My nose wrinkled. "Practice? Why?"

"You might be great at a lot of things, but this sword is unlike anything you've handled. If you're not careful with it, the weapon will be your downfall instead of your road to victory," she said, making the situation feel more ominous than I saw it.

"Right. Let's go then. No time to waste." I grabbed on to both Olida and Ivy, teleporting us back to the hut. When my feet touched the dirt, I was face-to-chest with an armor-covered fae and almost fell on my ass until a large hand wrapped around my waist, keeping me upright.

Normally, our magic kept us from teleporting too close to anyone or anything. Yet, somehow, I was snuggled up real close to a giant. My eyes scanned the armor-covered chest in front of me and moved their way to his face.

He had longer hair that fell in soft waves around his chiseled face—strong jawline, kissable lips, and a perfect nose all sat below swirling azure eyes that had me entranced.

"Lucinda, I presume?" he spoke, words like butter as a mischievous smile formed. Holy hell, this man was delicious.

I was yanked from his hold, and the spell the newcomer had over me broke while my bond with Finn flared to life. My poor mate was shaking with fury, so I turned around, running my hands over his chest and arms before cupping his face and forcing him to quit glaring at the mammoth of a man behind us.

"Yours, Finn. I'm all yours," I said sternly.

His forehead pressed against the top of my head. "I know, I just don't like…" He didn't have to finish. I understood his thoughts without needing to hear the words. I kept our faces close, holding his stare until his breathing evened and I didn't have to worry about a jealous mate.

I turned back to the others, still staying with Finn to make sure his emotions didn't get the better of him again. I didn't need him going all caveman on the hottie when I was pretty sure said hottie was Victor and could probably squash Finn within an instant.

"Did I forget to warn you that Victor has a certain appeal to him?" Olida cooed as Mosi held on to her.

"I think you conveniently left that out, but good thing I'm immune to it," I replied, smiling up at Finn, hoping like hell that was the case.

Victor smirked and cupped his ear when I looked back at him. "Then, why is your pulse accelerated?"

Oh, he was going to be trouble, and for once, I wasn't looking forward to it.

"Because I'm with my mate," I replied without missing a beat.

Victor nodded at me, then at Finn. "I see. My apologies."

Mosi moved toward the feathered fae with crimson wings. "You should get out more, so you don't overwhelm the rest of us when you decide to show your face, old friend."

Victor smiled, showcasing two rows of perfectly straight and white teeth. "You, of all people, should know I would only get worse. "

"This is true." Mosi sighed, then turned to me. "Lucinda Morrow, this is Victor Du Pont. He's older than even me if you'd believe it."

I nearly choked. "No, actually I don't." Where Mosi was wise and wrinkled, Victor was sharp and muscled.

Victor winked at me. "Part of my special ability. Lucky me."

Gods, I was really glad he didn't come out to play often.

Finn scoffed behind me, and I cast a glance at Olida and Ivy. Olida was openly admiring Victor, her eyes tracing every inch of the imposing fae. Ivy, on the other hand, was looking squarely at the ground with a tense Maddox behind her.

They really needed to get their shit sorted out before tomorrow. We needed all the capable hands we could get, which reminded me that I hadn't seen Neva yet. I wasn't sure if she was capable any longer, but I did need to check on her just as soon as we were done here.

"Where are the others? Do we need to worry about running into them?" I asked.

"While I respect my brothers and sisters, none of them can do what I do," Victor said smoothly.

I didn't even want to know what he meant by that. The more he spoke, the less hot he got. I was all about a confident man, but there was such a thing as overly confident.

"Right. Are we done here then?" I asked, enjoying the look of indignation that passed over Victor's face.

Mosi grinned. "I guess we are. I just wanted the two of you to meet. Everything else can wait until tomorrow."

"Not everything." Olida coughed, trying to hide her words.

Mosi ushered her back into their hut, likely before she could embarrass him more.

Victor studied Finn, then glanced back at me, shaking his head. "It's such a pity."

Finn lunged for the feathered fae leader, but Victor vanished before my mate could get hands on him. "I'm going to kill him."

"Now, now, Finnigan. There's no need for that." I spun him toward me, kissing him willingly in front of others for the first time.

Ivy groaned. "That's disgusting. Please, don't ever do that again."

I pulled back from Finn and smiled at her. There were several things I wanted to say, but then I remembered she was my mate's sister and none of them were appropriate.

"This has been an eventful day. I thought Olida wanted to take me to Yury, but I guess that's going to wait for a bit. I need to see Neva." My eyes met Finn's. "I'd like to do that on my own."

He nodded. "As long as you stay away from Victor, I don't care what you do."

"He might be easy on the eyes, but he's got nothing on you. His kind of cocky doesn't quite do it for me." I turned so the others couldn't see me slide my hand over his impressive length, emphasizing my words. "I'll see you back at the hut shortly?"

Finn cleared his throat. "Make it quick."

"Want us to keep you company, brother?" Ivy asked as I stepped away to call for Neva and didn't listen for his response.

Her name echoed through the trees as I stepped into

the shadows. If she hadn't come back yet, then I didn't imagine she wanted to be seen by anyone else.

Another minute passed before I opened my lips to call for her again, but I saw her ebony curls shine in the moonlight first.

"Neva," I said.

"Lucy."

CHAPTER 13

*N*eva stayed back, watching me cautiously. She was reserved, yet powerful in her own right. Her honey eyes had a golden glow to them, and her normally dark skin shined under the moonlight piercing through the trees.

"You're different," I said, moving to her side and leaning against a tree.

"I am. I went back home for the first time in much too long."

Her words surprised me, but I waited for her to elaborate before saying anything. Neva had only mentioned brief moments of her past before, and if she needed to get something off her chest again, I wanted to be there for her like she'd been there for me.

Another minute passed, and I started to think maybe I'd read the situation wrong. "Did you come to say goodbye?" I was beginning to notice an indifference about her that made me feel like things had irrevocably changed for her.

She shook her head. "No. Well, not in the way you mean."

I let out a soft laugh. "Care to explain?"

"I can't work for you anymore, Lucy. My job here is done. At least, the one I started out with. It's time for me to take my own advice and slay some of my past demons. Killing those creatures, taking lives... it was the first time I'd done so in almost a century. I used the power I'd tried my damnedest to forget I had, but that was wrong of me."

"Which part?" I asked. Given who I was and what I'd learned about myself, knowing what she thought was wrong was nearly as important as the thought of her not being around anymore. I'd grown to respect Neva and trust her judgement. Learning this gave me an insight to her I didn't have before.

"Honestly? Me pretending I was someone other than who I really am. I shamed you for it in my own ways, yet I was doing the same thing. I'd been so certain I'd changed that I didn't think twice about it, but being here, seeing you transform, I knew I had to do the same."

Gods, that struck me exactly where I thought it would, but still took me by surprise somehow. I adored who Neva had been around me. She was smart, thought before she acted, and had a calmness about her I'd never known before letting her in. The elf was everything I was not. I didn't want her to change, selfish as it was, but I understood her as well.

"What does that mean?" I asked before I began jumping to conclusions, at least verbally.

She sighed, snapping her fingers and sitting on a bench that hadn't been in the trees mere seconds before. "The me you've known, the me I've shown you the last few weeks, those are all parts of me, but not all of who I was before. I omitted my reasoning for going to work with the council before."

I strode over and sat next to her with a smile on my face. "Neva, you don't need to be ashamed about your choices to protect yourself. If you want to keep that part of your life buried, then I respect that. Don't feel guilty for the choices that made you feel safe."

She stared out into the trees, laughing quietly. "Nothing made me feel safe back then. I needed more knowledge, more of everything. I went to the council under the guise that I wanted to work in their library, but I was using them until I found my out. When I learned what our ancestors had done to the elven people... I lost it. I came home as soon as I could and attacked our elders."

Her eyes lost the glow I'd seen when she first arrived, and I knew she was seeing the past, so I stayed quiet while she gathered her thoughts.

"They were stealing our power for their own greed, but nobody knew I was the bastard child of an elder. My mother had hidden me until she could lie about my age. I had bloodline access to the elder's power, and I used it to destroy the hell they created."

I nudged her. "Closet badass was a fitting nickname, then. I don't see what's so wrong with that. You did exactly what we're trying to do here."

Neva turned her gaze on me, a fire in her eyes that I'd never seen before. "When I took that power from them, used it to destroy the corruption within our land, I couldn't contain it—I wasn't strong enough. The magic had to go somewhere and, when I unleashed it, I decimated half our village."

Damn. Neva had acted on emotion, and it was a big reason why I'd kept mine off for so long. Figuring out how to shut down my feelings was the only good thing I'd learned during my time in the castle.

"Shit happens, Neva. You made a mistake, and, if I know you, which I think I do, you've spent the last century paying the price for it," I said, hoping to make her feel better.

She grunted. "Killing those creatures reminded me of who I was, what I'd done. I had to go home and see what had happened to the people left. I might have destroyed the evil there, but I'd left them in shambles like a coward."

"What happened when you showed up?" I asked.

She smiled for the first time since appearing. "Well, they didn't throw stones at me."

"So, what's with the depressed mood? I know you've had to relive the past, but if they didn't try to kill you, why are you leaving us?"

Neva reached for my hand, magic tingling along her skin. "Do you feel that?" I nodded. "That's the power of my people. When I killed the elders, I technically became one. None of the elves could strip me of that power without me being present. Given I'd hidden, I took a piece of home with me, literally.

"When I showed back up, the new elders immediately knew I was there. I was circled and almost killed on sight, but my mother came as well. She's surprisingly risen in the ranks since my departure. I had also feared I'd killed her, or gotten her killed, but I wasn't brave enough to go back and find out."

"You punished yourself for more than you were responsible for, Neva," I said sternly.

She nodded. "In that, you might be right. Anyway, they didn't try to harm me. Instead, they allowed me to have a reunion with my mother before I explained pretty much everything that I'd just told you. They'd already figured out who my father was, so it made things a little easier."

"And they want you back?" I asked.

"They do, but I told them I had to finish what I started here. I will be present for the fight. I will use my power when necessary. After that, I will go home to the countryside in England that I once called my village and be with my people again."

As much as I hated those words, they also made me damned proud. Neva had come a long way since I found her in that alley being tortured. Now that I'd learned more about her, I assumed she'd been hoping for death back then. I'd taken that from her and given her a new purpose. I would miss her and everything she taught me over the last few years. More importantly, the way she pushed me to be someone better than I believed I could be.

"Do they allow fae into your village?" I asked with a grin.

"Not normally, but I think I can get them to make an exception for you," she replied, leaning her head on my shoulder.

"I'm going to miss you driving me crazy."

She laughed. "I'm not going to miss you driving me crazy."

"Lies," I teased.

We stayed quiet for a few minutes before she sat back up, turning to face me. "Did you meet the feathered fae?"

"Yeah. Be glad you didn't. Victor, apparently the only one we'll officially meet… he is something else."

Neva raised a brow. "Care to expand, or are you going to wait until I find out for myself? Is he another Yury?"

"Worse. I don't know what he is, but he's delicious to look at and sneaky. Something about him… I don't think he's bad, but I have a feeling he likes to toe the line. Which surprises me, given he hides away from the world. At least that's what Mosi thinks. Now that I say it out loud, I have a feeling he leads another life those closest to him have no clue about."

"Delicious, huh?" she asked.

My head shook, and I fought a smirk. "Out of all that, delicious is the part you ask about? You really have changed."

"Going home reminded me that I'm not getting any younger. I've been alive almost two centuries. Elves might have long lives, but I should probably consider my future a little more seriously now."

I stood up. "Well, for now, let's consider only the immediate future. If you're really comfortable still fighting with us, we leave tomorrow. First, I need to get the sword from Yury, though."

"Should we get the others? How is Ivy doing?" Neva asked while getting up as well.

"She's fine, actually. Olida worked some magic on her, and Ivy is back to being who she was before. Though, Maddox is overthinking things and trying to ruin what they have so she can find her true mate. A bunch of blah, blah, blah stuff that I'm sure you can ask her more about if you want."

Neva laughed. "You've changed, but not all that much. It makes me happy."

We both walked back toward the huts, and I realized I was happy, too, for the first time in… maybe forever. Sure, we hadn't killed Zephyr yet, but I had allowed myself to let people in. While I had more to lose now, I also had more to fight for.

When I'd first stormed Zephyr's castle after killing Edgar, I'd been okay with dying. I didn't have anything I believed worth sticking around for. I was reckless and careless and let myself be emotional.

While I cared about more now, I also saw the bigger picture. I'd grown enough to not be as selfish with my choices. We would finish this the right way or try again. I didn't want to see anyone die just to get my way.

"We're going to be okay, Neva. The both of us," I said as we got back to Mosi and Olida's.

"I think that's the best thing you've ever said."

I brushed her off as I knocked on the sealed door. I had considered waiting until the morning, but I wanted to see Yury tonight.

The wood glowed and the door opened as Olida peeked her head out. "Good to see you, Neva. What can I do for you ladies?"

"Did we interrupt something?" I asked with a chuckle.

Olida's hand brushed stray strands back from her face. "Uh, no."

"Right," I teased. "Where do we find Yury and the sword? I figured you might want to come with us, but you seem otherwise occupied."

Her cheeks darkened. "He should be in his cave. Did you check there already?"

"He wouldn't let us see where he lived the last time we were there," Neva said.

Olida laughed this time. "Makes sense. Well, if you can wait until tomorrow…"

I wrapped an arm around Neva. "Come on, Elf. Let's go yelling for him in the forest."

Neva sighed, and Olida grinned.

"Thanks, Lucy!" she called as we walked away, and

I tried to pretend that I had no idea what was going on behind the closed doors.

CHAPTER 14

Finn, Maddox, and Ivy found us before we got too far away and convinced us to eat dinner before we went and upset the not-witch.

"Fine, but there better be alcohol with dinner," I said.

Finn wrapped an arm around me. "Of course, dear."

I shrugged him off even as the bond flared within my chest. "No touching in public."

"Then, I get extra touching in private," he whispered low enough that I hoped no one else heard.

Before I could respond, he squeezed my ass and went to walk with Maddox. He didn't often show a playful side, and each time made my pulse quicken with excitement.

Ivy and Neva joined me as we headed to Ivy and Maddox's hut where there was apparently food. I was a little put out by this fact, because we didn't even have drinks in ours.

"Well, you didn't ask for anything extra, did you?" Ivy said after I grumbled my complaints.

"Whatever. I didn't ask you earlier, are you going with us to the castle tomorrow night?" As far as I knew, Ivy wasn't a fighter. She was supposedly over what had been done to her, so I wondered if she still needed closure—also known as revenge in my book.

She nodded "I am. Maddox tried to convince me otherwise, but this started with me and I want to be there when it's over."

I laughed. "Sorry to burst your bubble of importance there, but this started with me."

Neva sighed, moving between the two of us. "Both of you are wrong. Evil was created in that man long before either of you were born. You're both just pawns in the game he's about to lose."

I wouldn't argue with Neva. She was right. If it hadn't been me, Zephyr would have found someone else to train and turn into this weapon like he'd planned to do with Maeve, if she was to be believed.

We arrived at their hut and, sure enough, they had fresh breads, fruits and veggies, plus soup that Ivy heated up. I was officially jealous, and if we came back to the island after tomorrow, I'd be asking for food first.

I filled up on potato soup and sourdough bread while sipping on a fruity wine I wasn't fond of, but it was all they had. Apparently, Olida kept the hot toddies to herself when she wasn't passing out pots of it to me.

Finn leaned back in his chair next to me and groaned. "I'm ready for bed."

"I don't think so. You said food, then searching for Yury. I'm not going back to our hut until I have my sword in hand," I said with arms crossed.

He raised a brow at me. "You do realize it's not yours. We will destroy it after you use it to kill Zephyr."

I loved that he said when *I* killed the bastard. He wasn't going to try and be a macho man and take my moment away just because I was a woman. Finn respected my power and strengths, and that made accepting him a whole lot easier.

"Yeah, yeah. Details. Who cares about those?" I said flippantly.

"Apparently, not you," Maddox droned.

I pointed a finger at him. "You shut your mouth. You were supposed to stop being depressing to be around once we got Ivy back. Quit thinking about the future and *what-if*s. You're allowing them to ruin your present and missing out on one hell of a time by doing so."

Maddox's eyes widened, and everyone else was silent as I stared him down. I'd already had it out with Maddox more than once. I wasn't afraid of his temper or outbursts. Someone needed to give him a solid kick to the balls and I was happy to do it.

He took an annoying amount of time to comprehend my words, but when they registered, it was like a literal light went on in his eyes as they brightened. Maddox turned to Ivy, grabbed her cheeks, and kissed her passionately while mumbling apologies we couldn't really understand.

"Well, I've had enough of that. How about we find Yury?" Finn asked, already moving to stand.

"I'd love to argue and make you uncomfortable, but I actually want to find the oaf, so let's go." I grabbed on to Neva's hand and pulled her out the door with Finn right behind us.

With the three of us outside, I headed for the trees. "Should we yell 'Marco' and see if he's in the mood to play?" Both of them looked at me like I was crazy. "Human games. They're funnier when you're bored."

Neva grinned, and Finn just shook his head at me.

"I'll find him," Neva said as she pushed her hands out, silver sparks slithering around her fingers.

I couldn't see her magic beyond her hands, but I could certainly feel the pressure of it against my skin as I gave her some space.

Neva walked forward, and Finn asked, "Are we supposed to follow?"

"Well, I'm not being left behind, so yes," I answered, pushing him ahead.

We trailed after Neva for about twenty minutes before we came to a moss-covered hill. "Here," she said with bright golden eyes.

I pointed at her face. "Do your eyes always do that when you use magic?"

"Maybe." She grinned before turning to the hill and throwing a rock at it.

"I thought Yury was staying in a boulder," Finn said.

"Yeah, a boulder covered in dirt and moss to help keep it hidden," Neva replied just as a red door formed in the earth and a very angry Yury stepped out.

He stomped toward Neva, sniffing the air like a shifter as he got closer. His ire turned to curiosity when he faced Neva. "Where did you go?"

"Home," she answered proudly, staring up at his imposing height.

Yury inspected her for another minute before I got bored. "So, can we come in, or are we going to stand out here all night being impressed with the closet badass?"

Yury glared at me. "You are not welcome in my house."

"Oh, come on, Not Witch. Don't be an ass. We're just here for the sword," I sighed.

He laid eyes on Neva again, making me step closer to her.

"I won't hurt her, Hulk," he grumbled, noticing my movements.

"I know you won't." I grinned, implying a threat, except it wasn't from me. Neva was perfectly capable of taking care of herself.

Yury huffed. "Fine. Come inside."

We followed the sorcerer through the red wooden door and into the cave-like house, and my eyes immediately landed on the sword. It was laying on a coffee table, and I moved toward it, then paused. For the first time, nothing in me was called to the weapon.

"I can't sense any magic from the blade. Did it not work?" I asked.

Yury sighed. "I'm beginning to think none of this is worth it."

"Worth what?" I asked as he reached for the sword.

"Nothing." Yury shoved the hilt at me. "Test."

I raised a brow. "On you?"

"If you want to go outside, sure. I'd crush you like a bug. Or you can use this." He snapped his fingers and a ballistics dummy appeared at his side.

Neva stepped forward, touching the gel-like skin and snickering as she did. When she stepped back, the blank face had been turned into Zephyr. "Practice should be as real as possible." She shrugged.

"Gods, I'm going to miss you," I said, receiving an interesting look from Finn. "I'll tell you later," I added before stepping within striking distance of the fake Zephyr.

The sword still looked the same: long silver guard, black grip, and matching silver pommel with a sleek double-edged blade. Using both hands, I twisted the sword around, noticing it was lighter than before.

"Did you change something about the make of the blade?" I asked Yury, trying to find differences.

"No, it's just not weighted down with dark magic anymore."

Finn and Neva backed up as I nodded and took my first swing. The weapon moved fluidly and struck the dummy's chest like it was made from butter before I pulled back.

"Not sure I'll be able to practice for long unless you

have more of these," I said, watching as blood pooled within the gel where I'd struck.

Before anyone could reply to my comment, magic from the sword became evident as the tip dripped crimson and I turned to Yury. "I didn't remove the block. What happened?"

"I made a slight modification to your plan. The spell is blood activated. The only downside is that it can be used on anyone," Yury replied, but I couldn't see a downside to that.

The addition was ingenious, and I had to admit would be helpful to make Zephyr's death quicker. As much as I wanted him to suffer, I had no plans to toy with him.

Maybe I'd stop giving Yury such a hard time for being a rude recluse. These little details showed how much he did care, even when our fight with the king had nothing to do with him.

"Thanks for this" I raised the sword toward Yury.

He nodded and grunted before turning back to his desk and grabbing a bottle. Yury tossed it to Finn. "This is the poison. If Hulk decides to use the sword on someone else before finding Zephyr, you'll need to put no more than three drops of this on the blade for it to work like she wants again."

Finn tucked the bottle into his back pocket, and I huffed. "First, don't talk about me like I'm not standing right here. Second, why not just give it to me?"

Yury cracked a smile and snorted.

"What?" I asked, but he just walked away.

Neva stepped to my side and patted my arm. "Only three drops, Lucy. This poison isn't to be messed with. No offense, but you don't have the best track record with listening."

"Whatever." I snatched the new sheath I saw laying on the table and secured it around my waist. "What now?"

Neva glanced around. "You've scared Yury off, so I guess we go."

"Not scared," Yury's voice sounded from a distance, but we still couldn't see.

"Not scared, not witch… I wonder what else he is not," I jeered, already having forgotten I'd considered being nicer to him. It was hard when he made things so easy to poke at. A part of me was convinced he actually enjoyed it. If he didn't, he likely would have left the moment he saved Ivy.

"Not patient," Yury grumbled as he stomped back into the room.

I pointed to his feet. "Be easy on those sandals. I think they stopped making them a couple decades ago."

Finn wrapped a hand around my mouth. "I'm pretty sure he's trying to help us. Let's not upset him."

I shrugged since his fingers were still over my mouth, and Yury came back in the room with a bottle of pills. "I worked on these for the fae. Give them to Mosi." He handed them to Neva.

"You're leaving?" I asked, but my words were muffled by Finn's fingers, so I bit him and asked again.

"Not yet, but I won't be fighting," Yury answered.

"You made me bleed," Finn muttered at the same time.

I ignored my mate and focused on the not-witch. "You know something."

He shrugged. "I know lots of things."

I shook my finger at him, stepping closer until I was in his personal space and poking him in the chest. "That might be true, but you know something about this fight. What did Mosi tell you? Why are you still here? I'd love to take credit with my winning personality, but something tells me there's more."

Yury lowered his head, towering over me with magic pulsing from him. "Back off, Hulk."

"Or what?" I challenged.

We stared at each other for an uncomfortable amount of time, but I wasn't breaking first. Yury would have to cave or accept he had a new houseguest.

"I have an investment in the outcome of this battle," Yury finally said with a sigh.

"Which is?" I asked.

"None of your business. Now, get out of my house before I force you out." Yury crossed his arms and stepped back.

I had no doubts that the sorcerer had set up precautions that would allow him to do just that, as if we were vampires not welcome across the threshold.

"Fine, but the less you tell us, the less chance we have to win," I said.

Yury glowered at me. "Who said it was better for me if you won?"

Well, shit.

$\mathcal{Y}$ury wouldn't give up anything else before kicking us out. He tried to play like he wasn't on our side, but I wasn't buying it. Sure, he might be getting something out of all this, and I wasn't sure what, but he wasn't hoping we'd lose. Not after the things he'd done to give us a leg up in the fight.

Neva went back to her pocket realm after promising me she was okay and would see me in the morning. Finn and I stayed in for the rest of the night, getting enough sleep and mentally preparing for the following day.

I wasn't stupid enough to believe the fight to kill Zephyr would be easy. All of us needed to be at our best, and that meant full stomachs and rested bodies.

As soon as the sun rose, I was out of bed and dressed in all black. It seemed fitting for the occasion. My favorite tight corset was wrapped tightly over a lace long-sleeve shirt that seemed fragile but was the next best thing to the suit I'd ruined before. The lace was made of the same strong spider's silk my last fighting outfit was made from, but it lacked the stone material to really make it protective.

My leather pants were spelled to withstand most sword strikes, but not dark magic. I'd still need to be careful, given we had no one on the inside to tell us what kind of magic the guards would be attacking back with.

Just as I tied my hair into a braid and wrapped it into a bun, Finn's warm hand settled on my lower back. "Are you ready?"

Finn was wearing black cargo pants and boots with a dark grey tee that matched his charcoal eyes. He had a couple of daggers poking out of his pockets and appeared even more ready than I was.

"Just need to grab the sword," I replied, walking away from the mirror to the kitchen counter where I'd left the blade the night before.

The sheath was attached to a thin leather belt, and I looped it around my pants before adjusting where the sword sat.

Finn openly appraised me. "I hate that you're going to be in danger today and there's nothing I can do about it."

I stalked closer to him, placing my hand on his chest. "You're doing everything I need by not trying to pretend I'm some damsel in distress, and standing by my side. If you want any chance of me moving forward in life, then just keep remembering how much I need this."

His forehead pressed to mind. "I know, and I'll be right at your back the whole time."

"Not when I fight Zephyr. He will use you against me. It has to be just me and him, Finn. Promise me," I demanded. Zephyr wouldn't be fighting clean, and Finn would be a distraction to me. I cared too much for him. It was why I'd fought my feelings every step of the way.

"I will do my best. I believe you can beat him in a fair fight, but we both know things might not go in our favor. If you're not doing well, I will be there, no matter the consequences," he replied, and I nodded.

It was the best I could ask of him. I might not love him like he said he loved me, but I still felt the same bond. The need to keep him safe. All of it was overwhelming and because of that, there was a lot we couldn't predict about the coming fight. Emotions were going to be high, which made things dangerous.

We headed to Mosi and Olida's. When we arrived, the door was open, and we walked right in. Images of Olida's cheeky grin from the night before surfaced, and I smirked at her glowing face. "Good night?" I asked.

"Nothing like facing death to make you live a little," she said with a wink, and that was enough for me.

Victor was standing next to Mosi in the living room. He inspected me and shook his head. "Such a pretty thing like you shouldn't be wearing a sword at her side."

I smiled sweetly at him. "Would you like to go outside? I'm even prettier under the sun." My words were kind, but based on the glower in Victor's eyes, he heard the threat.

"Where did you find her again?" Victor asked Mosi.

"She was born right here on Fae Islands. Dark Fae parents as predictable as they come," Mosi answered.

I glanced up at Finn who was glaring daggers at Victor. "It's okay, Finnigan. He might be hot, but he has no appeal to me," I whispered.

Finn nodded, the glare disappearing, but not his tension.

"So, group training and then we're off to see the wizard?" I asked, and everyone in the room looked at me in confusion. "Spend more time on Earth and that would have made sense."

Neva silently entered the hut, appearing at my side. "Maybe we'll find your heart, Tin Man."

"Ha. Ha. So funny," I deadpanned as she grinned.

"You two are very odd sometimes," Finn said.

I fist-bumped Neva. "He said only sometimes. I'd call that a win for the day."

She sobered, glancing around the room. "Too bad it wasn't the only one we needed."

"Speaking of, we should head to the training area," Mosi said, dressed in varying shades of brown leathers that gave him a camouflage sort of appearance and fit him well.

Olida followed after him and Victor as they shuffled by us, and I raised a brow at her. "You're training?"

She chuckled. "No, dear. I'm observing and making sure none of you overbearing fae hurt yourselves before the real fight."

We trailed after her out the door as she skipped ahead to join Mosi again. They held hands like the disgustingly adorable old people I used to see around the park when I took walks back in LA.

Thinking of that made me miss the simplicity of the few years there, but I knew it was an empty life. I still didn't want to stay in the fae realm when this was all over, but I also had no regrets about my decision to come. It had changed my life in more ways than I could have ever predicted.

I tossed my arm over Neva's shoulders. "Thank you for being here and putting up with me."

"Someone had to," she said with a wink.

I laughed. "One trip back home and you're full of sass."

She grabbed on to my hand draped over her shoulder. "I should be thanking you as well. I was ready for life to be over when you found me. I had nothing left, and you gave me a purpose, Lucy. I won't be able to ever repay you for that."

"It's not about repaying anything. You're my friend, Neva," I said, trying not to imagine what could happen to her during the battle if we weren't careful.

Neva had shown several times that she was more powerful than I'd known, but still, I had a hard time not picturing the timid elf I'd always known being tossed into a deadly battle with no chance of survival.

"And you're my friend. No matter what. Everything is going to work out just the way it's supposed to. Don't worry about anything else other than staying alive," Neva said, and Finn grunted.

He didn't like talking about any of this. I tried to have several conversations with him about what might happen during the fight, but he'd deflected each time. I didn't blame him. He wasn't raised the same way I was. Even though I knew Finn was strong and capable, he wasn't a warrior at heart. He was a protector, and to me, there was a huge difference.

Most importantly, Finn hadn't denied me of being who I was, and I wouldn't do the same to him.

The training area Mosi had mentioned was just a clearing in the middle of the trees opposite the beach I liked to frequent. There were already dozens of fae present, all of them fighting in groups until one of them whistled and, like a well-trained militia, every one of them turned, stood up straight, and faced us with their heads held high.

Warriors of all shapes and sizes stood before us. Men and women alike, tall and short, wide and thin. There were no two alike, and I admired that.

True to Mosi's word, there were no other feathered fae present besides Victor. As Mosi and Olida went forward to address their people, I leveled my stare on Victor. "Why do you and the others hide from everyone?"

"Greed is a powerful thing, Ms. Morrow. Most of us have lived long lives and spent time with others, learning the hard way that you're either the leader when you have abilities like ours or you're the prey. Most of us don't want to be either. We just want to live our lives," Victor answered.

"I've been neither and still lived my life," I countered, even though I understood what he meant. If Zephyr had been able to get his hands on more of the feathered fae, he would have attempted to command them like he'd done to me. Staying out of the spotlight wasn't such a bad thing.

He tsked at me, shaking a finger. "That's not true, and you know it, but we're not here to hash out how we all choose to live. My people showed up when it mattered, did they not?"

I shrugged. "I wouldn't know. I haven't seen them."

"Point well made. When you do, you'll understand. While it's not my place to tell you about them, I can advise you to pay close attention. You just might learn a thing or two. Maybe we can even tempt you to come spend some time with us in our sanctuary," Victor offered with a wink. Just when I'd thought we might have a whole conversation without some sort of lewd comment.

Finn flinched at my side, but I stepped in front of him as I spoke. "Victor, I'm not like you and the others. I never have been, and I never will be. I don't know what your power is, but I assure you it will never be strong enough to lure me in."

He glanced at Finn's hold on my waist and nodded.

"I see that, but it doesn't mean we can't have our fun on the side."

Finn finally had enough, and I decided not to stop him, considering my mate had been patient enough already. He lunged for Victor, pulling one of the daggers from his side pocket. "I don't care how powerful you are or what you can do. If you speak to my mate in any other manner than respectable again, I will cut you to pieces."

One of Finn's hands wrapped around Victor's neck, ready to choke him while the blade Finn held pressed into Victor's skin just above his hold. It wasn't enough to draw blood unless Victor made any sudden movements. They locked stares, and it was several seconds before Victor responded.

"There is the mate I'd been hoping to see. You just might be worthy of her after all."

Finn's grip tightened, making Victor gulp and a drop of blood appear. "What is that supposed to mean?"

"If you loosen your hold, I just might tell you," Victor mumbled. "Or I could make you and keep the secrets to myself."

Finn made a grumbling sound before pushing Victor back and tucking away the dagger. "Speak with respect or I won't hesitate next time I go after you."

"I never meant any disrespect," Victor began, and I rolled my eyes with a sigh. "Well, it didn't start that way," he corrected.

"Then, what did you mean?" I asked once Finn was back standing with me and Neva.

"When Mosi told me of your existence, I was intrigued. You're the only female feathered fae and the only one of us who is neither light nor dark. Do you know how many hearts you broke when we learned you'd mated with someone not like us?"

I crossed my arms. "Well, maybe if you left your hidey hole, the rest of you could have found mates by now as well."

Victor nodded. "I see that now, but I also needed to know that the fae chosen for you was worthy. You might not understand the significance of your existence, but you are hope for the rest of us. If we can remove Zephyr from his throne, more than our leadership will change."

My fingers drummed over the sword at my side. "Zephyr will die today, and Finn is more worthy of me than I am of him. If you'd have taken five minutes to speak with him instead of annoying me and antagonizing him, you might have learned that without getting a dagger to the throat."

Victor laughed. "What fun would that have been?"

Mosi and Olida came back over to us before the conversation could take another wrong turn. "The other fae will keep with their training, and we will stay over here," Mosi said, unfurling his silver feathered wings. It was the first time I'd seen them since the fight with Edgar, and I'd forgotten how magnificent they were.

"Are you finally going to show me why all these crazy fae follow you, old man?" I joked.

He shook his head with a smile. "I'm going to show you why you should stay out of this old man's way when he's in battle mode."

Without giving any other warning, Mosi threw a hardened feather at me that lodged into my corset. "Alright. Let's see what you got," I said, letting my own wings out and hoping the others stayed out of our way.

CHAPTER 16

I was never again going to call Mosi an old man. He'd kicked my ass more than once, and I'd learned new things about my wings from both him and Victor, like how to extend only one of them if necessary.

After Finn's earlier threats, Victor did indeed remain on his best behavior during the training and even helped my mate with his own fighting, along with Ivy and Maddox who joined us about halfway through, looking much happier than the day before. Though, I didn't get to interact much with them between Mosi's and Neva's attacks.

Working with Neva had surprised me the most. I'd never spent any time with elves before her. Their kind were even more segregated than the fae, though they lived on Earth, so I was constantly in awe of the things she was capable of. Not only was Neva smart as hell, but the more she used her powers, the quicker and stronger she became.

By the end of the day, the elf was running circles around me, and I almost handed her the sword. "You know how many times I could have used your help when we were assisting the witches and shifters?" I asked through heavy breaths as she threw magic my way that I was barely managing to dodge.

Neva grinned. "I do, but then you wouldn't be as capable as you are now. I would have done something if I actually thought you were in danger."

I rolled my eyes and willingly caught a blast to the chest, falling back onto the grass.

Olida appeared in my line of sight as I refused to get up. "While training is always good, we still need you to function later. How about we call it?"

She reached a hand down, yanking me up with more force than I was ready for, and I nearly brought us both back to the ground.

"Oops." She grinned as I stood on my own.

"Right. We can call it as long as there is food involved in whatever is next. I need to eat before we leave or I'm going to be hangry," I said as my stomach grumbled.

"I assume that's another one of your odd human phrases, but yes, I have a feast prepared back at the huts. Everyone is welcome," Olida said before disappearing.

I turned to see Neva was already walking off and

Finn was laughing with Victor. "What are the two of you up to?" I asked as I joined them.

"Nothing," they both said at the same time.

"Right. Well, while you're here doing nothing, I'm going to go eat." I disappeared and arrived at the huts to find Olida hadn't been kidding about the feast. More tables than I'd seen in their village were placed between all of the huts, and there was a buffet of foods. Soups, salads, breads, fruits, and so much more. It was a vegetarian's dream come true.

I was the first to arrive and wasn't polite enough to wait for anyone. Neva arrived at the same time as Finn, Victor, and Mosi, except she appeared to have run back, smiling with a pride I was glad to see.

As soon as I got my food, Olida appeared at my side and hooked her arm through mine. "Join me?"

I glanced at Finn, and he nodded, so I agreed without feeling like I needed to tell him I was disappearing. I hadn't spent much time with Finn during the day, but something told me waiting a little longer to see him would be worth it by spending a few moments with Olida.

We entered their hut, and she closed the door. "I feel like I'm in trouble," I teased.

Olida grinned, but it didn't quite meet her eyes. "Not at all, but there are things you need to know before going into this battle."

I sat my plate on her kitchen counter, frustrated it no longer looked as appealing as it did before she'd said those words.

"What do you know?" I asked gruffly.

"Mosi hasn't been as forthcoming with his visions as of late, so technically, I don't *know* anything, but I have a strong intuition and I believe you should be warned. Mosi is adamant that the future not be messed with, but I've grown to care for you as my own, Lucinda. I don't want to see you revert back to the person you were when I first met you."

"You're not making me feel any better, Olida. *What* do you know?" I repeated my previous question.

"This is a battle, and you're a smart woman. You're aware people are going to die, but do you really understand what that means now that you've grown to care for others?" she asked.

My fingers wrapped around the edge of the counter, and stone cracked under my hold. "Who is going to die?"

"Like I said, this is only my intuition. I don't know anything for certain, but I want you to think about what could happen. Not to scare or anger you, but to prepare you as I know you have been doing to Finn. Grief brings even the strongest to their knees, and you are not above that kind of anguish. I want you to understand that you can't save everyone, and that does not make their death your fault."

My heart pounded in my chest as I tried not to picture the lifeless faces of Finn, Neva, Ivy, Maddox, and Mosi.

"Will you still feel that way even if it's your mate I can't save?" I asked with a bite in my words.

She nodded and reached her hand out to me, squeezing my palm. "I've lived a long time, Lucinda. I know how the world works, and if it's my mate's time, then so be it. I would not let anger and blame tear me down."

"Then you're a stronger woman than me," I said, knowing I would tear the world apart in rage if Finn died in the battle and I couldn't save him.

"We will see about that, but my intent wasn't to cause you concern. I want you to know I will be here waiting. This island is a safe place for you, and I will do whatever it takes to help you, should you need it."

A feeling that had never come over me began to suck the breath from my chest as I stared into Olida's lavender eyes. She was everything I'd hoped for in a mother while growing up, everything I never had. I was a grown woman now, but I couldn't help the deep-seated need of wanting all the things a child should have had.

Olida came toward me as if she'd been able to read my thoughts. She pulled me away from the counter and wrapped her arms around me. "Everything is going to be okay, Lucinda. Trust that whatever happens was meant to be and don't look back. Focus on your future, because I believe that if you allow it to be, whatever lies ahead for you will be bright."

I hugged her back, soaking in the warmth of her embrace and letting my guard down. "Thank you, Olida," was all I could say without worrying about my emotions getting the best of me.

She was right about all of it. I needed to find a way to be the warrior Zephyr trained me to be while keeping the humanity I'd learned from all the people who were about to fight by my side. Each of them had taught me something, shown me the world wasn't as bad as I tried to believe.

Olida pulled back. "Now, eat your food. We don't waste around here." She smacked me on the ass like I was a child needing swatting.

"Yes ma'am, but let's join the others. I'm sure both of our mates would prefer our company," I said, picking up my food.

"Look at you caring about what others think," she teased as we walked out the door.

"Yeah, yeah. Just don't tell anyone else."

ANOTHER HOUR LATER, WE ALL HAD FULL STOMACHS, AND the sun was just beginning its descent. Our time was up, and everyone was ready to leave. Murmurs sounded through the gathered crowd as everyone waited for Mosi to give his final pep talk.

Neva stayed close to me and Finn, then Ivy and Maddox joined. Each of us was strapped with additional daggers and as ready as we could be. Those who didn't have special outfits like I'd kept for myself wore armor over their chests, but even I knew that wouldn't keep them safe for long if they weren't at their best.

Finn kept hold of my hand as I turned around, sensing someone watching us. Yury was in the shadows; the last glimmer of sunlight reflecting off his bald head was the only thing that gave him away. I didn't know what he was hiding for, but I said nothing.

It wasn't the time to concern myself with his actions, especially when I heard Neva yip in pain.

"What's wrong?" I asked.

She reached into the back pocket of her pants and pulled out the bottle of pills I remembered Yury giving her. "Crap. I was supposed to give these to Mosi."

I chuckled, turning back to call Yury out, but he was already gone. "Hand them to me," I said, already knowing who would get it done in the quickest time possible.

Neva reluctantly handed the bottle over, and I teleported to Olida. "Mosi was supposed to give one of these to all of the fae fighting with us, except he didn't get them in time. I'm assuming you can take care of it?"

She nodded. "What are they?"

"No idea. They came from Yury. Assuming he doesn't want us all dead, I imagine they'll do something to help us," I said.

"Alright, then." She shook out five clear pills and handed them to me.

"What's that for?" I asked, backing up.

Olida raised a brow. "Are you and your friends exempt from Yury's help?"

I snatched them to avoid an argument. "Fine, but no promises they'll take them." Then, I disappeared.

Everyone was still where I'd left them, and I shoved my open palm into the center of the group. "Your choice if you want to take one."

Maddox was the first to reach in. "Yury saved Ivy. I don't think he'd try to kill us now."

Ivy went next, then Neva. Finn glanced at me. "What do you think?"

"That I'm tired of having other people's magic inside me, but it probably won't hurt if you want to take it," I said honestly.

"Fair enough." Finn watched Maddox since he was the first to take the pill. Nothing happened, not to him or Ivy.

Neva wiggled, stretching her arms out. "It's some sort of shield magic. I can't get a good read on it, but it's like Yury was trying to create something that would act as armor and hide our magic all at the same time."

I took the pill meant for Finn and shoved it toward his mouth. "Take it. Now."

He grinned, plucking the capsule from my fingers before I could shove it down his throat. "If it will make you feel better." Finn swallowed it and then eyed me. "You're next."

I almost argued that I didn't need it considering Yury had already hidden my magical scent when we first met and I had my spider's silk, but he was right. I didn't need to be *that* stubborn.

Swallowing the pill, I choked on its vinegar taste. "That was horrid."

"I'm sure you've had worse things in your mouth," Neva said without thinking, and then covered her mouth as Finn growled at her.

I offered her a high five that she didn't take, then Mosi began to speak, likely using magic to amplify his voice, considering we heard him clearly from fifty yards away.

"Thank you to everyone for being here. I know some of you have been waiting years for this moment, and I'm proud to have you all fighting at my side. Tonight will not be easy. I won't sugarcoat things and pretend lives won't be lost. You all are making a great sacrifice that won't go without acknowledgement.

"I've just been told my better half has given out a pill magically created from the sorcerer who has been a guest on our island. Please make sure you've taken it and know it will only aid our attempt to keep everyone as safe as we can for as long as we can."

Olida stepped next to him, telling me she was done handing the capsules out, and I hoped everyone listened to her and Mosi. Though, something told me Olida's threats were already enough to convince them.

"From here, we will teleport to the castle and separate into the groups we sorted during training. You all know where you're to go. If you are fatally injured and can teleport out of the fight, do so. Olida and some of the others will be here waiting to heal those they can. Do not be stubborn."

Mosi's stare met mine as if he'd said the last bit just

for me. I grinned in response as he narrowed his mahogany eyes before continuing.

"What about the meeting with those from outside of our island? Who will lead once Zephyr is dead?" a man from up front asked, but I couldn't see who he was.

Mosi sighed. "Unfortunately, not everyone could be present that deserved to be there for the meeting we had planned. As of now, it still stands that the next leaders will *not* be decided by who is the strongest or most powerful. Instead, once we know where we stand after the battle, we will schedule a date for pulling a number of fae from each island and take nominations. At that point, it will be up to the people to decide."

I hadn't heard anything about these meetings, but then again, I'd made it pretty clear that I wanted nothing to do with the throne after Zephyr was dead. Surprisingly, it did make me feel better that they'd been working on what came after.

Mosi paused, giving his people the opportunity to voice more concerns, but nobody else spoke up and he was back in warrior mode.

"Tonight, we earn our freedom and safety back. Tonight, we end the terror that has ruled our world for too many decades. Tonight, we take the crown back!" Mosi chanted loudly, and shouts rose from the gathered fae.

The amount of optimism was contagious, but after speaking with Olida, I didn't quite feel their level of excitement. Instead, I focused on the image of me driving the sword into Zephyr and watching as the realization set in for him that his own creation had become his downfall.

It was the only way this day ended with any kind of success, and I couldn't think of it turning out any other way.

CHAPTER 17

We teleported to the beaches of West Island just beyond the castle. The warriors were spread out, and there were about fifty of us in total. I wasn't sure if that would be enough, but it was more than I expected when I had first pictured breaking down the castle walls.

Finn squeezed my hand. "Are you ready for this?"

"I am. Zephyr is going to die." Those words had been on repeat in my head for most of the day. I was convinced if I thought them enough that nothing else would stand in my way of making sure it happened.

"I'll be right there making sure you have the opportunity to finish this," Finn replied.

"Me, too," Neva added, her eyes taking on the golden glow again.

Ivy and Maddox were there, too, but they wouldn't be with us. As much as I would have preferred keeping our group together, Mosi said he needed more leaders for the others. Maddox volunteered, and of course Ivy wanted to stay with him.

Finn released me to go speak with her. He was nervous about her part in all of this. She wanted to help even though she wasn't an experienced fighter. The little bit she'd learned on the island wasn't really enough to keep her alive, but if she stayed with Maddox, she thought she could at least heal people or help teleport them out as needed.

Just like when she had accepted the fate of dying when I killed Zephyr, I was okay with this, too. We all had purpose, and I admired Ivy for not being afraid of hers. She might not be tied to Zephyr anymore, but she was still a healer and would do a lot of good during the fight if she was kept safe.

It was almost time to break into groups, and Ivy came back over to us with Finn and Maddox. She hugged me tightly. "No matter what happens, I'm really glad you said yes to my brother and came back."

"Thanks, Ivy. Listen to Maddox and stay safe. I don't want to deal with Finn or Maddox if you die. It was enough when you were kidnapped," I said with a wink.

Ivy smiled in return as she pulled away and went to Neva next. Maddox stood next to me and Finn while they said their parting goodbyes.

"Are you good?" Finn asked Maddox.

He nodded. "I hate to say it, but once again, Lucinda shook me out of my idiocy. I have a lot to fight for. This isn't the end."

I smirked but said nothing in response. I could gloat

after this was all over and we were far from here on a beach without a psycho fae waiting to be killed.

Maddox left with Ivy once she was done, and Mosi joined us. "The two groups going through the front will do their best to get you a path inside the castle, but I expect you all to help make that happen as well. This isn't just about you," he said.

Past me would have taken offense to that, but I knew what he meant. I didn't need to be reckless when dozens of fae were putting their lives on the line to fight whatever was waiting for us.

"Got it. Shall we?" I swung my arm out toward the direction of the castle, and Mosi nodded.

The other groups had already moved out, and we were the last three left. As we moved into the trees and followed the path to the castle, my adrenaline increased, and I shook my wings out. I had been saving up feathers, taking a couple new ones as the missing ones grew back. Besides my magic, the feathers would be my primary weapon of choice.

Finn held one of his daggers in hand with his wings out as well, and I could sense his magic waiting to burst. He was tense but kept his composure.

Neva didn't put off any worries. In fact, I was concerned she was too comfortable. I knew she'd been growing back into her powers, but I hoped she was smart enough to understand how unpredictable dark magic was. The closer we got to the castle, the more I knew it was going to be a problem.

A heaviness settled over me but didn't slow my

steps as we trudged forward. "Do you feel that?" I asked.

"Everyone be ready at a moment's notice to defend yourselves," Mosi replied as his only answer.

The walls came into sight. A few holes were still present from when I'd first arrived to kill Zephyr. It was just a few short weeks ago, but it seemed like forever after all that had been happening.

The sky was dark already, and the castle had no lights on, welcoming us as if they knew exactly when we'd be attacking. This made me nervous, but I didn't say anything. No breeze blew in from sea, and I wondered if we were already within the shield that was mentioned before.

The first group made it to the front gate, and we all heard a grunt, followed by the thud of someone going down. I had no clue if it was a warrior from our side or one of the king's guards, but it was the signal everyone needed to charge in.

"Stay close to me for as long as possible, please," Finn said as he cast one last look my way and we ran toward the entrance.

"I promise to do my best." I gave him a squeeze on the arm before we were inside the walls, tension radiating off of each of us.

There were at least twenty fae dressed in the king's blue colors, and the fae by the gate that lay on the ground bleeding from his neck was not one of them. Mosi stopped and pulled the unknown fae outside of the castle walls before following back after us.

One life lost and the fight hadn't even really started. That was not good, but we couldn't let it stop us. We were already here, and it was too late for anyone to back out now.

Three fae came at us while Mosi and Neva went ahead to help others. I turned to Finn. "Beat you to the third one."

He shook his head as we charged on. "Only you would make a game out of killing people."

I didn't have time to defend my reasoning. Instead, I flung one of my feathers toward the closest fae and grinned as it sank into his shoulder. Finn took on the other guy, and a woman was left between us, trying to decide who to tag team.

While Finn was exchanging magical blows with his opponent, I was busy going for the neck of the dude in front of me. I had added a burning magic to the feathers I'd been storing, so while the fae was distracted with trying to pull it out of his skin, I used my wings to propel me forward and snapped his neck.

I turned for the woman whose eyes were wide, and she was trembling. While she stood there, another fae came at me—a male with blood in his eyes. I disregarded the woman and dropped low as the newcomer flew for me.

As he sailed over me, I used another feather to cut into his leathery wings and enjoyed the roar of pain a little too much as he stumbled to the ground.

"You bitch. I'm going to kill you," he grunted.

"Those words are like music to my ears," I cooed.

Before he could charge again, Finn was behind him and stabbed the guard in the back so forcefully that the tip of his dagger came out the other side. "Don't play with them, Lucinda," Finn chastised.

I ignored him and turned back to the woman. Upon closer inspection, I took in her tangled mousy-brown hair and pale face. She held up shaking hands. "I don't want to fight you. I just want to find my son and get out of here."

Finn and I shared a glance. Normally, I wasn't one to let people go in a fight. It went against everything I'd believed in, but this woman had several chances to attack and didn't. It might be dumb, but I was feeling kind.

"I can't say we'll offer your son the same mercy if he comes at us, but we won't follow you if you run out that gate," I said and still she didn't move.

"I won't leave without my son." Her brown eyes hardened as she stopped shaking.

I took a step away from her and closer to Finn. "Do what you want, but I suggest changing out of those clothes if you're going to wait around. We see that color, we see the enemy"

Neither Finn nor I waited for her response. With our wings behind us, our feet pounded on the dirt ground. The fight had already moved through this area, and dead fae lay scattered around us. Not wanting to let any weaker emotions in, I avoided looking down as I eyed the gates that would allow us into the castle's main area.

Fae were fighting in small groups as we moved along, but nobody at first glance seemed to need our help. Mosi asked us not to charge right in for Zephyr, but if the fae were handling themselves, I wasn't going to wait another moment.

"Which way?" Finn asked.

I couldn't see anyone we knew, but on my third glance around the castle, I noticed two of Mosi's warriors in trouble beyond the door that would lead to what I wanted most. My hesitation only lasted a split second before I pulled Finn toward the others who needed our help.

Dark magic swirled heavily in the air, and the closer I got, the more I realized we'd made a mistake. The fog rolling from the one guard they were trying to take down was tangible and began choking me. My steps slowed, and I couldn't see Finn anymore as my vision tunneled.

These fae had been beyond help, and I'd fallen right into the trap. Son of a bitch.

My fingers clawed at my throat as my skin began to burn. I wanted to scream, but no sounds would come out. I felt pressure at my back but couldn't concentrate long enough to figure out what it was from.

My knees finally buckled, and I fell to the cobbled ground. I had just enough strength left to keep my eyes open and saw another fae charging for us. I wanted to wave them off, but my muscles wouldn't move. Whatever this was, it was stronger than the shield pills Yury had given us.

Neva's golden glow shone brightly as I helplessly watched her charge for the fae putting off the deadly magic. She wasn't at all affected by it based upon the speed in which she passed me. I couldn't keep my eyes open any longer and closed them, listening for sounds instead, but even my hearing had been tampered with.

Another minute passed, and I was rolled over, Victor's face coming into view. "Finn?" I asked, needing to know where he was.

"Neva's got him, and he's fine. Just stay still for a minute," Victor growled as I tried to get up quicker than my body would allow.

His crimson wings came out and wrapped around me. "No, Victor," I objected, thinking he was being inappropriate again.

"Trust me, Lucinda," he demanded, while bringing my body closer to his. A warmth spread through me as my muscles relaxed and the heaviness I'd been plagued with lifted.

When I could hold my head on my own, Victor loosened his grip. As soon as I sat up, he went to Finn and did the same thing to him. Watching from the outside was interesting as Victor's crimson wings turned almost black before shimmering as his whole body shook.

I hadn't felt him tremble, but there was no denying it as he held Finn. Waiting for Victor to finish felt like an eternity, but I stayed out of his way as Neva came back to me.

"How did you stop that fae?" I asked.

"Like Maeve, that one hadn't anticipated an elf coming for him, but he's taken care of now," she replied stiffly.

"Are you okay?" I looked her in the eyes, wanting a truthful answer.

She nodded. "I'm fine, I promise. Now, let's get inside that castle. They have things mostly under control out here now that all the feathered fae arrived."

Glancing behind us, sure enough, I could see that our numbers had increased. Well, maybe stayed the same. I couldn't see nearly the number of warriors we arrived with. The feathered fae shimmered as they moved, their speed unlike anything I'd ever known. Suddenly, Victor's offer to have me train with them didn't seem like such a bad thing.

Finn getting up pulled my attention back, and I went to him. "Thank you, Victor," I said earnestly. "I'm assuming your abilities Mosi wouldn't tell us about allowed you to heal us?"

"Healing, luring people in, cloaking my magical presence. All just a part of my everyday life," he replied.

"Right. It is better that you don't get out much," Finn said, glancing around our surroundings, and I agreed with a nod.

Victor grinned at the three of us. "Maybe. Now, don't you have a king to kill?"

That I did. We'd done our part out here. It was time for the real fight.

CHAPTER 18

Finn and Neva followed me as we raced for the castle doors. Zephyr hadn't shown his face outside, so that left me to believe he was hiding in his throne room. Magic built within me, and I pushed it out, waiting for his guards to try to stop us.

I took the stairs three at a time, practically flying up them with Finn right behind me and Neva doing her best to keep up with her shorter legs. As long as she was in my peripherals, I had no intention of slowing down.

"Where are we going?" Finn asked when we got to the top of the stairs.

"His private chambers. Best case scenario, there are only a handful of guards and he's in one of his aging fits like Maeve told us about," I said without missing a beat as we continued to run. Then, I realized the fact we hadn't been stopped yet wasn't normal and probably wasn't a good thing. I slowed my paces.

"And worst case?" Finn asked as Neva caught up to us.

"There are another dozen or more guards waiting for us and Zephyr is in his best form, which is the most likely of scenarios," I replied with little emotion.

"Should I go back and get help?" Neva asked from next to me as I nearly came to a stop, knowing we only had one more corner to go before we'd know what we were dealing with.

"It's too late now. We'll be fine. Just go in using magic instead of hand-to-hand combat." I pulled several feathers from my pockets and handed a few to each of them. "Don't poke yourselves with them. You'll regret it. And don't miss. This is all the extra I have left."

Neva rolled her eyes at me and handed her feathers to Finn. "There isn't anyone that should be innocent up here, right?" I shook my head. "Then, I don't need any help."

I raised my brows at her. "You sure?"

"I've done some of my own training. I'm very sure," she replied as we came to the last corner.

I stopped them both. "Zephyr is mine. Depending on how many guards are there, I will either help you or go straight for his door." I patted the sword at my side. "This is the only thing I believe will kill him if he's at his best. Nobody try to be a hero and help me."

Finn grabbed my corset to pull me closer, and we heard shouts down the hallway. They knew we were here, so our time was running out, but apparently, my mate didn't give a damn.

His lips crushed down on mine, then jerked back. "Don't be a hero, either. We need you alive more than we need him dead."

With a pounding heart that had nothing to do with fear and all to do with passion I never expected to ever find, I nodded. "Let's go kill some more fae."

Finn gave me a reason to live, and his kiss reminded me how much I wanted a lifetime of that. I wanted the happiness I never thought I deserved before. I wanted a life without fear. I was so close to grasping it. So damn close.

With weapons in hand, I led the way around the corner confidently. There was no more running, no more rushing. The fae waiting for us were going to see what strength looked like before we even touched them.

Neva was like a star next to me, throwing off light and heat that wasn't at all comforting when I got too close to her. Finn's wings were out, and he held feathers in one hand with a dagger in the other, ready for any kind of attack as magic sparked around his hands.

I stood between them both, teal swirls moving around my body and wings, caressing me like a lover and strengthened my every move. My hair was still back in a bun, and I could see clearly around me with no distraction as ten fae waited for us to act first.

That was their second mistake. Their first was even being here at all.

"Now," I hissed as I sent a blast of magic out to the fae closest to us while searching for Zephyr.

The door to his chambers was closed, but the metal cut-out I'd seen before was open, making me assume he was listening, and possibly even watching.

Dark magic collided with all three of ours, but nothing as strong as what we'd experienced outside of the castle. Unsurprisingly, Zephyr chose the wrong guards to be his final line of protection.

Finn began throwing feathers; one missed its mark, but the other two hit their intended targets, one in a fae's chest and the other in a different guard's neck. That one made even me cringe as blood spurted onto the ground. He couldn't even scream from his vocal cords being damaged.

Neva was already inching closer to the guards without waiting for me or Finn. She moved swiftly and with purpose, her light growing brighter with every burst of magic she let loose. On closer inspection, I noticed that her ears also became more pointed, something I'd never seen on her before.

But I couldn't just watch any longer.

The guards split up, and most of them came at me and Finn, while only a few took on Neva. Her size made them choose incorrectly, and I grinned while frying one of the incoming fae with my magic and stabbing a feather into him as he fell at my feet. The hits might not kill him, but he wasn't getting up anytime soon.

Finn was fighting two others and handling them

fine, so I made sure to watch my own back. Last time I faced Zephyr's guards, I was broken and angry and not thinking for myself. I had been ready to kill him or die, but that wasn't the case any longer.

I was a new me, and I felt the power of being my true self rise to the surface. "Zephyr! Get out here and fight me like the king you're supposed to be," I yelled, hoping to taunt him into opening the door as I used my hardened wings to cut into the chest of a guard who tried to sneak up behind me.

With several of the guards down already, I didn't feel guilty about trying to get through the door and leaving Finn and Neva on their own. Especially when Neva was taking fae down every chance she got without missing a beat.

Another wave of guards arrived, making me hesitate, but Finn nodded for me to continue on as he and Neva readied for another attack.

Calling on power deep within me, I sent a stream of magic at the open hole of the door before I stood in front of it. I heard a grunt, but by the time I could see inside, Zephyr was nowhere in sight.

Using my fist, I pounded on the door. "Come on out, Zephy. It's time to play." With every impact my hand made, the door cracked. I changed my tactics and kicked below the handle as hard as I could.

The metal door groaned beneath my power, so I repeated the movements three more times before backing up and then ramming into it with my wing.

I stumbled into the room as the lock gave out to find

Zephyr smirking in the corner and a sword swinging for my head that I managed to duck away from just in time.

"Lucinda, meet Dante—Gabriel's replacement," Zephyr said, acting like the coward I should have always known him to be.

I really wanted to pull my own sword out, but Finn was the only one with the poison, and I couldn't just walk away for a refill after I finished Dante. Instead, I kept my wings at my side and prepared to fight with no real weapon as the brute of a fae came at me again.

Deflecting the next hit, my wing went up, but the sword pierced right through it. Shit, that had hurt.

"Don't play with her, Dante. Kill her!" Zephyr shouted as I recovered and made the next move.

I was out of feathers with the burning magic on them, but I could still use my regular ones, freshly plucked. I pulled two more, uncaring where they came from or if they left a bald spot. I sent one of them flying toward the fae while I kept the other in my hand and rammed my shoulder into his stomach before sinking the second feather between his ribs, aiming for a lung.

Dante wheezed, confirming I'd hit my mark, but it didn't slow him down. "I'm not easy to kill," he sneered, and I laughed.

"Funny. Zephyr must have made you believe that one, but something I've learned is that we all have a weakness and I'm going to find yours," I said, really wishing I could use the sword, but instead, I called on my magic and thrust both of my hands toward the fae.

Dante crashed into a cabinet, unmoving, and I began to smile in triumph until I was stabbed where my wings sprouted in my back. Searing pain radiated through me.

"I won't let you take another one of my men. Thanks to you, I learned women were too emotional for what I wanted. Dante has been a nice addition," Zephyr taunted as I turned toward him.

My wings were limp at my sides and completely useless to me after Zephyr's blow. "Apparently, you've decided to fight like a coward, hitting someone with their back to you."

He smirked. "Didn't you learn anything in your time with me? All is fair in war, Lucinda. What I don't understand is how you overcame the magic. You left here last time exactly as I wanted you."

I remembered Ivy saying I'd become exactly what Zephyr wanted, but he clearly hadn't known we had Yury. While I didn't appreciate the sorcerer's bedside manner, I was more grateful than ever to him in that moment that I wasn't what Zephyr expected. Something told me his plan had been counting on me to be tainted with dark magic.

"Wish I could say I was sorry, but I'm not," I said, sending a bit of power his way and testing him. Pity he wasn't in one of his aging fits.

"I should have known you'd remain a disappointment. Your own parents didn't even want you. They'd wanted me to kill you. Did you know that? I saved your life, and now I'm going to take it like I should have back then," Zephyr said, having chosen his words carefully.

Words that reminded me of the mental torment he used to put me through. Words that used to make me think he loved me like his own child. Words that manipulated me into becoming a monster. Words that no longer had an effect on me.

"What's worse? You're not even half the same fae I made you into. I sense nothing from you. No strength besides what's coming from out there, but even your friends aren't coming to your rescue. Even they don't believe you're worth saving," Zephyr taunted as he lashed out at me again with his power.

Electricity wrapped around me, and my muscles seized. My eyes slammed shut as my jaw locked. A warmth built from my core as I concentrated on who I was. Zephyr never bothered to get to know the real me, the me who he thought wasn't good enough. I now knew otherwise about myself.

His magic was burning my skin, but mine was counteracting it. As my power grew, I felt myself relaxing, fighting from my heart instead of anger like the mother tree had taught me, but I wasn't quick enough. Dante had gotten back up and slammed into me from behind. His massive arms wrapped around my upper body, cracking my ribs.

Damn it. I would not die here. I wouldn't give Zephyr the satisfaction of my death.

Yet, even with all the magic I'd been building, I

couldn't make my wings move. I couldn't get my arms free.

A roar sounded from the door just before my head slammed into the edge of Zephyr's desk. My vision faltered, but the hold around me had been released, and I wouldn't give up. I gave myself a mental smack and used the desk to help me stand.

Finn was fighting with Dante, and I wasted no time reaching for the sword. The hilt warmed in my hand as I limped toward Zephyr. "You're going to die."

He laughed, loud and joyous. "There are only two things that can kill me, Lucinda, and you are not one of them. Neither is that sword. I made that for Gabriel. Do you think I'm stupid enough to give someone a weapon to kill me? It won't even hurt me long enough for you to see me bleed."

While he was going on about how smart and powerful that he was, I'd inched closer. Close enough that I was within striking distance.

"As enlightening as this conversation has been, I think I'm done with you." I didn't have as much strength as I would have liked, but that almost made things easier. Zephyr believed me to be weakened, and he'd kept his guard down.

He had one hand resting on his hip as he spoke, giving me the opening that I needed. I surged forward and jabbed the sword between the armor he wore, through his armpit.

"Did you really think you would stop me?" he asked with a laugh.

Zephyr shoved me back, the sword still within my grasp. Shit. Maybe I should have left it in his chest cavity. Or maybe I'd been wrong with my idea, and the spell I asked Yury to do wouldn't work.

Zephyr stalked toward me, and Finn was still fighting with Dante. He wouldn't make it back to me in time to help.

"Always the disappointment, Lucinda." Zephyr stalked toward me, shadowy magic seeping from his skin as he readied for a killing blow.

I lifted the sword to strike first, and the blood still on it caught both of our attentions as it turned black and bubbled along the blade.

Zephyr stared at it, confused, and I didn't wait for another opportunity.

My wings twitched at my sides, finally coming back to life after having been stabbed earlier, and I swung the sword at Zephyr's head, hoping to take it clean off, but his arm came up, taking the impact. He roared as his twitching hand thudded to the blood-soaked carpet.

"What did you do to me?" he screeched. His arm began turning grey, and instead of blood dripping from the open wound, it boiled at the stub.

Confidence settled into me that the spell was working, just slower than I'd expected. "I gave you back what should have only been meant for you," I replied, standing up straighter when I felt Finn at my back.

Zephyr fell to his knees. The rest of his exposed skin began smoking, and black ooze dripped from his eyes, ears, and the wounds I'd made. The king I'd once admired and thought I loved as a father suffered for several minutes as I stood above him just watching.

My eyes stayed on Zephyr's until he rolled to the ground, no life left in his broken body.

"You did it," Finn said.

That wasn't good enough for me, and my strength had come back. At least enough that I felt sure about my next move.

I stepped forward, bringing the sword back up, and bent my knees as I brought the blade down with full force onto Zephyr's neck. The metal cut bone with little resistance, and blood splattered back at me as Zephyr's head rolled several inches away from his body. His golden crown clattered against the hard floor.

Using my magic, the crown floated into the air and I clenched my fingers into a fist. I'd hated that crown and all Zephyr had thought it stood for. With a squeeze, the metal snapped into pieces before falling back to the ground.

Even then, I didn't feel satisfied. I wanted to cut him into pieces just like his precious crown was, then burn everything. I moved to strike again, but Neva came storming in, interrupting my murderous actions.

"Bring his head, and let's end this fight before more people die," she said quickly, blood trickling down her neck from her ear.

Using the sword, I jabbed it into Zephyr's head. "I'll bring this if someone burns the body. We can't risk him coming back somehow."

There was a fireplace behind Zephyr's desk that wasn't burning, but that changed with a bit of magic from Neva. Finn hauled Zephyr's body up and tossed it into the flames, kicking Zephyr's legs in when it looked like he wouldn't fit.

The smell of burning flesh wafted through the room as dark smoke began to rise from the fireplace. Satisfied that was enough, I followed Finn and Neva out the door with the sword resting above my shoulder and Zephyr's head still at the tip.

I'd done what I had come to do. Now, it was time to end the war Zephyr had started.

CHAPTER 19

We arrived back outside to find the feathered fae battling against Zephyr's guards, along with only a handful of the warriors who had arrived with us. Gods, I hoped at least most of them were just injured and not dead.

Maddox and Mosi appeared to need the most help. "What the hell happened out here?" I asked as we ran toward our friends.

"I don't know. I came down as soon as I saw Finn didn't need my help. Zephyr's guards were almost defeated when I went back to you. They must have caught their second wind," Neva replied.

Finn took the sword from me, giving me time to object, but I didn't. I'd had my moment. He could have this.

He raised the sword in the air and yelled, "Zephyr is dead. Stand down or join him!"

A good portion of the fae stopped, but not all of

them. A few even grew more agitated and fought harder against our people.

"I've got Mosi. The two of you help Maddox," Finn said, giving my hand a quick squeeze as he darted to our right, sword still in his hand.

Neva stayed at my side, keeping pace with me this time since my injuries were preventing me from moving as fast as before. My healing was already kicking in, though, and I wasn't afraid to face more of the guards.

Ivy was nowhere to be seen, and I assumed she was off helping the injured fae, considering Maddox wasn't going insane.

The two fae fighting Maddox saw us approaching and nodded at each other. I pulled more feathers from my wings and flung them as quickly as I could, but it wasn't fast enough. Before my feathers could hit their marks, the two fae worked simultaneously and pulled blades from behind their backs.

One guard charged left and the other right. I saw what they were going to do, and I teleported the remaining thirty feet, hoping to get there in time. I roared, using both of my wings to come down on the two fae, but the damage was already done.

Each of their knives had plunged into Maddox's neck, and he was laying back on the ground. Neva burned me with her power as she flung the treacherous fae away and followed after them. I stayed with Maddox, trying to keep him conscious.

"Come on, Maddie. I need you to stay awake. I'm

also really sorry if this hurts." I grimaced as I pulled the blades out and covered his wounds with my hands. I'd never healed an open wound, just brought people back from the brink of death. I'd saved Maddox before, though, and I would do it again.

"Ivy," he gurgled.

"Don't talk." I scowled as even more blood seeped between my fingers.

Neva came back to me. "Oh, Gods," she cried.

"Why isn't he healing?" I asked as I pushed magic into him.

A scream sounded from behind me, and my heart broke. Ivy appeared at Maddox's head. My eyes met hers and I needed no words to hear pleas.

"Come on, Maddox. Help us heal you," I said with force as I moved my hands away from the wounds and let Ivy take over.

Maddox didn't respond this time as we both worked on him.

Using my palms, I pressed hard onto his chest. When that did nothing, I tore at his armor until I got to exposed skin and tried again. I didn't intend to stop. I couldn't. Maddox had to live.

Then, I saw Ivy was stroking his face and there was no more blood coming out.

"It worked?" I asked, full of hope until she looked at me again.

Her blue eyes were blinded by tears as she gave me the slightest shake of her head.

"No. This isn't happening. I'm not losing any of

you." My own eyes burned with tears, and I slammed my fist into Maddox again. "Wake up, damn it!"

I'd let myself care for him as a friend. We'd even understood each other when he'd been without Ivy. Maddox wasn't supposed to die. Mosi had seen him at the final fight. This wasn't right.

Mosi kneeled next to me. "I'm sorry, Lucinda. You can't save him."

My glare turned on him. "You knew?"

"I did. Maddox and Ivy saved a lot of lives. This was always his path," Mosi admitted, but it didn't make me feel any better.

I let the fury within me rise, taking over the grief as I shoved Mosi back. He didn't try to stop my movements as I followed after him.

"You could have said something. We could have made sure that…" I didn't know what, but we could have done something.

Just as I was about to strike Mosi with my wings, Finn wrapped his arms around me, cutting his own skin to save the fae that betrayed us.

"Lucinda, stop. Mosi chose exactly what Maddox would have wanted," he whispered in my ear.

"No, I won't accept that. Maddox *wanted* Ivy. We could have kept one of the feathered fae with him. Or made him stay on the island. There are always options," I yelled back, tears falling down my face.

"Options that would have led to a lot more deaths," Finn said, still holding on to me. I softened my wings.

"Did you know?" I asked, not sure what I would do if Finn had.

"No, but I know both Mosi and Maddox. There was no other option. I promise."

My head fell forward as the loss of Maddox continued to pain my heart. I turned my head and saw Neva consoling Ivy, still next to Maddox's body, then looked away. If I stared any longer, I didn't know what I would do.

When I pulled away from Finn, Mosi was already gone and the fighting around us was done. Victor strode toward us, bleeding from a singular wound on his forehead and looking better than anyone else I'd seen.

"It's over. A handful of guards surrendered, and the rest are taken care of. We won," he said.

I huffed. "Yeah, but at what cost?"

Victor peeked past me and nodded. "I lost one of my own as well. I'm sorry for your loss."

Gods, how many had died today? Could my heart even take knowing that answer? I wasn't sure and wasn't ready to find out.

Neva and Ivy joined us. I reached my arms out to Ivy, and she fell into them willingly, tears starting anew for both of us. Finn joined, and I tucked my wings away as he held us tightly.

The battle was finished, but it was far from over for those of us left.

A FEW DAYS HAD PASSED AS FAE HEALED FROM THEIR physical wounds, but the ones people couldn't see were what I worried about the most.

Finn stayed strong for Ivy as they grieved together. I tried to stay out of their way when Ivy came to talk or just be with us at our hut, but I still hurt, too.

I didn't know why. I knew Maddox, but I didn't care for him like I did Finn. He hadn't been in my life for years, only weeks. We were barely friends, but being unable to save him gutted me in ways I hadn't expected.

I couldn't even look at Mosi. While I didn't have the sudden urge to strike him anymore, I still wanted to scream in his face whenever he came around.

The blame landed with the both of us, and I hoped he suffered as I did.

"How are you holding up?" Neva asked as I sat on the beach, staring at the nothingness before me.

I shrugged. "Fine."

She sat next to me, nudging me with her shoulder. "You're not fine, and you need to realize that's okay. There's nothing wrong with being sad, Lucy."

My head whipped toward her so fast my neck popped. "I'm not sad, Neva. I'm angry. I'm guilty. I'm tired. I'm a lot of things, but not sad."

"I get that's how you feel now, and I understand all of it. I've been there. This is the first real loss you've ever had, but you need to understand it's not your fault," Neva said softly.

At first, I said nothing in return. My eyes stared at

the marvelous sunrise, the waves cresting in perfect synchronization, and the clear blue sky high above. Except, while my eyes saw all of it, none of the beauty registered with me as I tried to block out the worst of my thoughts.

"What is it?" Neva encouraged.

My head shook. It didn't matter that Neva was the best friend I'd ever had. I couldn't say what was plaguing me out loud. Not after all we'd been through. Not after all that was sacrificed to get there.

"Lucinda, I've been on your side for a long time now. I've seen a lot of things. Whatever has you scared can't be worse than anything from before," Neva added.

My laugh that followed her words was dark and husky. "From before? From the me I was when I didn't care? The one who would be dancing in the streets right now instead of wallowing in guilt? The me I wish I still was?" My voice rose with each question until I let go of the one thing I wanted to hide most.

Neva reached a hand toward me, but I jerked away and stood. "No. I don't deserve comfort. People died to kill the man who haunted me. Twenty-six of them from here, plus all the innocent fae on Zephyr's side who never should have been part of the fight to begin with but thought they had no other choice. 'Fight or die.' The king's motto.

"My need for vengeance got people killed, Neva. Lives were changed, families torn apart. I got what I wanted, and people suffered. How is that okay? It's not.

I'm still a monster. Except now, it's worse, because I care too much, and I don't know how to turn it all off," I practically yelled into the sky as more tears trickled down my cheeks.

My wings unfurled as my anger increased and power swirled within me. I shoved my hands in front of me and let it all go as I screamed out my frustrations.

The fight was over. Zephyr was dead. I was supposed to feel better, and yet, I was worse off than before. None of it was fair.

As my power died down, so did the tension rolling through my body. I turned back, and Neva was standing behind me.

"Better?" she asked.

"Not really," I replied.

She stepped toward me, taking my hands in hers as she spoke. "I can't take your hurt away, Lucy. I won't lie to you and pretend it won't always be there. What happened at the castle was life-changing, but only you can decide if it will change your life for the better or worse. What's done is done now, and none of those who died would want it to be in vain."

Her words registered with me. The first ones to really make sense since we'd left the castle.

Neva kept going when I didn't respond. "All of those fae knew what they were signing up for. Don't be selfish enough to think they were doing it for you and that any of those deaths are your fault. Each of them had their own reasons. Maybe it was safety for their family or a better world for their kids to live in. I don't know. None of us ever will, but they all made a choice. Maddox made a choice. He fought for himself and for Ivy. For all the hell they'd been through since she healed Zephyr. Maddox didn't die for you. He died for the love of his life."

The ache in my chest eased slightly as she spoke. Only Neva would have been able to get through to me, and I think we both knew it deep down. I wasn't okay by any means, but I wouldn't deny that I felt my inner rage easing its grasp on me.

"I'm going to miss you," I said, pulling out of her hold and tossing an arm around her before turning us both to stare at the open waters.

"Good thing we're supernatural. Distance isn't much when you can travel it within a blink of an eye," she replied, and I heard the smile in her voice without having to see it.

"We have a mess to clean up here, but you don't need to stay. We'll come visit you when we head back to Earth," I said.

She turned to me. "Are you really going back? Do you think that's where you and Finn would be most happy?"

"I don't know, but I know I need to go back to figure it out. Whether it's for closure or for good, I can't ignore the call to be back on Earth," I answered.

She grinned. "There's nothing wrong with leaving your options open. Just don't stay in LA for too long. That's a life you don't need to go back to. I'll drag you out of there myself if I have to."

I laughed, a happy sound, for the first time in days. "I don't doubt that for a second."

"Come on. Let's go see the others. They're going to announce the nominations for Zephyr's replacement."

My muscles tensed as Neva said the words. I might be feeling better about my guilt, but I wasn't sure I was ready for Mosi, Olida, and Ivy.

"Trust me." Neva held out a hand for me that seemed more like a challenge. A challenge to face the things I'd been evading since Maddox's death.

I accepted and teleported us back to the huts before she could say anything else, but nobody was there. "Where did they go?" I asked.

"They're not here. Mosi didn't want to lift the shield. I told them not to wait for us and promised to bring you. We have to head to North Island."

If she'd said West Island, I'd have refused. Going back to where all the carnage had taken place so soon wasn't something I was willing to do, but North Island was manageable.

We teleported once more and found a line of people on the beach walking down a path through the trees. We followed, and my nerves erupted once again.

As my steps slowed, Finn appeared at my side. He smiled at me, grabbing my hand and offering his silent support. I took it as he led us to the front of the crowd that had to include at least two hundred fae.

Mosi, Olida, Victor, and several others I didn't know stood on a wood platform. Once Mosi caught sight of us, he nodded at one of the others.

An older fae with greying hair stepped forward. "For those of you who don't know me, I'm Edson and here to represent the fae of East Island. We are all here today to nominate candidates for our new king or queen. It's time for our people to move forward and take back what has been lost inside this realm for too many decades."

Agreements rang out from the crowd and, as I looked around, I saw a fire in the fae people that I'd never known existed before. Never again would they let someone like Zephyr take from them as he had.

"East Island would like to nominate Mosi Albyn as our next leader," Edson shouted into the crowd as murmurs sounded, but I couldn't tell if they were good or bad.

A woman stood next. She was younger and a warrior, judging by the deep scar that ran down her left cheek. "I am Sheva from North Island and we, too, nominate Mosi Albyn."

My gaze went to Olida and Mosi. Olida was near having a panic attack, likely from having been forced off her protected island and from the two nominations.

Mosi moved to stand, but Victor pushed him back in his seat, whispering something before approaching the crowd. "While I and my people do not live within the fae realm, we hope to change that one day. The only way we will do that is if Mosi is your king. He is the most trusted fae I have ever met, and you would be lucky to have him to lead you."

The crowd grew silent as the South Island

representative also nominated Mosi. No one from West Island was chosen to speak, which didn't surprise me. There probably weren't many of them left.

Mosi stood, finally stepping forward, and before he began to speak, the crowd of fae began to chant.

"King Mosi Albyn! King Mosi Albyn!"

There was a peace that settled within me as Finn, Neva, and I joined in the shouting. Fae Islands would be better than it ever had. The people would heal, and somehow, we would all move on. Each of us in our own way.

With my toes in the sand and a drink in my hand, I was the happiest I'd been in... well, ever. It also helped that Finn was behind me as I lounged back against his warm, naked chest.

His hand slid over my exposed stomach, and I couldn't stop the shiver that ran through my body. "I really wanted to hate Earth, but I can't say I do," he said.

"I knew you wouldn't. There's a reason Fae Islands resembles this place."

We were in Hawaii on a black sand beach and watching a family of turtles shuffle across the shoreline of the deserted beach. The weather was a perfect eighty degrees, and I was relaxed.

It had been a long six months since I killed Zephyr. So much had happened, and everything had changed. Some things slowly and others rapidly, like when Mosi and Olida became King and Queen.

While he'd received the only official nomination, there was a waiting period of seven days before things became official. Olida had a hard time with the adjustment, but with the help of myself and Ivy, we had her settled in no time.

With Mosi and Olida as their leaders, the fae realm was slowly being rebuilt and, like I expected, it was turning out to be even more glorious than ever before.

We'd also found out that Mosi had promised Yury his secret island when they left. I'd wondered for so long why the sorcerer had stuck around, but it finally made sense when Mosi had relinquished the shield magic to Yury and, as king, given Yury permission to come and go from the islands as much as he needed, as long as he never brought trouble to the realm.

As my thoughts got away from me, Finn must have sensed my distraction and edged his hand further south until my hips flinched from the contact.

"Are you sure that's a good idea?" I asked, voice breathier than I would have liked.

"Touching my mate is always a good idea," he murmured against my ear before sucking on my lobe.

I moaned and leaned further into him, feeling his hard length against my back and wishing it was elsewhere *in* my body.

"They'll be here soon," I whispered, tilting my head back as Finn's lips worked their way down my neck.

"I heard you thinking too hard, and now you're not. I don't care when they arrive. I'm servicing my mate first."

Gods, I really did love him.

I'd yet to tell him with words. It was the only part of the old me I hadn't tackled, but the more he touched me, the more he loved me for who I was, the more I had to fight verbalizing how I felt.

I didn't know why I did so, and he didn't ever push me. Not even after saying he loved me a million times and me never once saying it back.

Finn's fingers stretched under my swimsuit bottoms, and his other hand played with my nipple until it hardened under his touch. I moaned louder than I'd intended and moved to straddle him until I heard voices.

"Did you hear that? I told you we should have waited at the house. I'm not going any further for fear I'll have to burn my eyes out," Ivy complained as I heard the soft sounds of Neva's laughter.

"Chicken," Neva called as she came around the bushes.

By then, I was scrambling up from next to Finn and apologizing to his lower half.

"We could have just teleported anywhere else and you wouldn't have to apologize," he grumbled, staying on the sand, likely until he had his erection in check.

The moment I saw Neva's ebony curls bouncing as she ran toward me, I forgot all about my mate's troubles. I met her in the middle and hugged her tight.

It had been three months since we'd seen each other. After seeing that Fae Islands was operating fine under Mosi and Olida's rule, Neva had gone back home like she'd planned, and I'd convinced Finn to see all the best parts of Earth.

He'd been hesitant to leave Ivy, but she was better every day and lived at the castle working with Olida on healing the people and bringing much-needed joy to the way things were run. Plus, I was pretty sure Mosi enjoyed Ivy's presence. It kept Olida's mischievous side in check when things got too out of hand.

Though, I'd been disappointed when both Ivy and Mosi had objected to the idea of a whiskey booth in the market. They complained about the potential for drunk fae running rampant all over the islands, but neither Olida nor I saw the problem with it.

When Neva pulled back, her smile shone brightly against her dark skin, and her honey eyes glowed with delight. "I've missed you," she said.

"I missed you, too," I replied before calling for Ivy. "I promise it's safe to come out."

She groaned, but came anyway, smiling wider as she got closer and throwing her arms around me. "Hello, sister. Sorry to interrupt the potential baby-making of my future nephew or niece."

My face lost all color as my arms fell to my sides. Baby-making? Oh, Gods.

Ivy laughed, stepping back. "Kidding, Lucy. Totally just kidding."

Neva pinched my elbow and zapped me with magic. "Snap out of it, woman. You can't get pregnant just from someone mentioning it."

"Don't even joke about that," I muttered at Ivy.

They both grinned back at me. "I see not much has changed," Ivy teased.

Finn joined us and held me from behind but kept his hands around my waist instead of where I'd needed them earlier. "Yep. You're still the annoying sister I've always had," Finn joked.

"I'm glad you both could make it. Next time, we'll come to you," I said, paying closer attention to Ivy and looking for signs of her grief.

For weeks after Maddox's death, Ivy's eyes were swollen and red to the point that I wondered if the tears would ever stop for her. Maddox might not have been her true mate, but their love had been deep.

We'd stayed long enough in Fae Islands to make sure she was okay and had a new purpose to keep her moving forward with Olida, but still, my own guilt hadn't quite gone away, and I worried about her often.

Except, she was perfectly fine standing before me. She stood straight, her eyes shined with happiness, and she smiled meaningfully at all of us. Seeing her helped ease the ache in my chest.

"We have a surprise for the two of you," Ivy said with glee and then whistled.

Considering we'd been on Earth for months, I half-expected a dog to come barreling down the beach, but instead, it was Mosi and Olida who materialized next to us.

Before I could really register that they were there, Olida threw her arms around me, yanking me from Finn's hold.

"Your soul feels so light," she whispered in my ear while squeezing tighter.

"How many hot toddies did you have before leaving the confines of the fae realm?" I asked, assuming it hadn't been easy to convince Olida to leave the safety of the castle.

She hiccupped. "Just a couple."

Mosi coughed. "Barrels."

At some point, I'd forgiven Mosi for keeping Maddox's death from us. I'd known why he'd done it. His gift came with a price, and I didn't envy the things he saw, but for a while, I'd let my anger lie with him. It wasn't fair, but like the true leader he was, Mosi had accepted the blame without complaint.

I hugged him next, an action that was getting to be easier for me to accept as the days passed. The image of Ivy throwing herself at me for the first time and how disgusted I'd been felt like a lifetime ago and made me laugh.

"What? Do I smell funny to you?" Mosi joked.

"Of course you do, old man. You smell of responsibility and adulthood, two things I hope to avoid for as long as possible," I replied, moving back to Finn.

Mosi pulled a piece of wood from his pocket and handed it to me. "Here. Ash asked me to give this to you."

My face scrunched in confusion as I reached for the oddly shaped present and saw a note attached. The moment my fingers touched the bark, I sucked in a breath and nearly dropped it.

Finn was reaching for the gift within an instant. "What happened?"

I waved him off. "Just an overreaction." The magic had taken me by surprise, but I recognized it now.

The longer I held the piece of tree, the easier it was to accept. Traces of the mother tree magic flowed through me and settled at my core as I unfolded the note.

Lucinda,

My children have healed, and the islands are thriving. I wanted you to know that the sacrifices made did not go unnoticed. Please, accept this part of me as a gift. One I hope you should never have a reason to use, but the power I have is yours to access now that I'm fully restored.

Please, stay safe and don't forget to come visit us.

With respect,

Maia, the mother tree

"What is it?" Ivy asked as Neva held her back while slyly trying to look closer as well.

I grinned at their curiosity. "A gift from the mother tree. A piece of her life force and something I hope we never have to use."

Mosi slapped a hand on my shoulder. "The world knows what you did. They know that you're unrivaled, just like we've always believed, Lucinda. Just focus on the present and living your life. For now, that's all that matters."

I nodded at him. His words rang true, and I smiled up at Finn. "Enough talk. How about we show you guys why we invited you here?" I said, ready to go for a swim with the dolphins.

Olida glanced around, eyes wide and the hesitation evident. "I don't think I'm drunk enough for this."

My arm looped through hers. "Oh, come on. I promise you're going to be just fine. I'll be by your side the whole time."

Her lavender eyes wrinkled at the edges, and she matched my smile. "Well, if that's the case, I should have come sooner."

I knew she was partially teasing, but the trust Olida had in me meant more to me than I'd ever be able to properly tell her with words. Instead, I shared a part of me that I hoped the others enjoyed just as much as I had: Earth.

THE FEW DAYS WE HAD WITH EVERYONE WENT BY IN A BLUR and much too fast. We'd hardly slept, drank way too much, and laughed even more. My heart was full, and the last of my guilt had vanished during the visit.

Grief was still there and always would be. It was part of living. Something I'd had to accept was that nothing was guaranteed, but what was the point of living if we didn't enjoy the good things while we could?

Living in fear made for a lonely existence, and I was done being lonely.

I'd gone from thriving off hurting others and keeping everyone miles away from my heart to allowing them all in and surviving off the love of those closest to me.

Finn and I stayed at the beach house in Hawaii after the others left that afternoon. Night had fallen, and I found myself standing on the deck overlooking the beach and ocean.

While I'd enjoyed every moment of our company, there hadn't been even one second of being alone for the three days.

Closing my eyes, I angled my head up to the moon and soaked in the ocean breeze, smelling the salty air while the sounds of nature quieted for the night.

Finn joined me, holding me tight in his arms as I kept my eyes closed.

"Did you have fun?" he asked.

"It was better than I could have imagined, except for one thing," I replied, turning around to face him.

He lowered his head to mine, kissing me softly before asking, "What's that?"

"We didn't get to finish what we started on the beach when they arrived." My hands roamed his bare chest before traveling to his waist where he was only wearing loose pajama bottoms.

Finn's hands fisted in my dress, pulling it up until

my ass was practically hanging out. "No, we didn't. I think you owe someone another apology."

I tossed my head back and laughed, and he took advantage before I could reply, kissing my neck, then down my collarbone and nipping at my shoulders.

My back arched against the deck railing as I let him love me, relishing in the fact that we wouldn't be interrupted this time.

With every caress and kiss he gave, my heart swelled. Even when he tangled his hands in my long hair and gripped the strands almost painfully until he had me positioned just where he wanted.

Finn always seemed to know exactly what I needed before I did. His touch freed every part of me that I'd kept locked away for so long. I loved him with everything I was, and as he devoured my lips, I couldn't keep it in any longer.

Using both hands, I gripped his face and pulled Finn back, smirking as he pouted at being stopped.

Holding his stare, I lost myself in his silver eyes and almost didn't say what I so badly needed to get out, but as his brow furrowed in concern, I had to ease his worries.

"I love you, Finn Barlow." The words I'd fought so hard to keep in flowed from my lips with ease, and Finn was back on me before I could blink.

He kissed me furiously before his hand pressed against my chest. "Your heart is the greatest gift you could ever give me. Now, I'm going to show you how much I love you in return."

Finn picked me up, and I wrapped my legs around his waist as he carried me back into the house to do just that.

He was the happily ever after I didn't know I wanted and everything I'd ever needed but thought I didn't deserve.

Now, I knew better, and I'd never forget my worth again.

This was only just the beginning for us, and for the first time in my life, I eagerly awaited what the future held.

Want a chance to see Lucinda and Finn again? Check out Luna Marked, the next series in my Mystics and Mayhem world!

Scorned by Blood

A New Adult Vampire series featuring a supernatural hunter and the sexy vampire bound to protect her no matter the cost.

Luna Marked

A complete New Adult wolf shifter series (dual POV) featuring a strong-willed leading lady and a patient, yet fierce alpha male.

Broken Court

A complete New Adult Urban Fantasy series featuring an unconventional and anti-heroine leading lady, a broody love interest, and a fae kingdom with a vile king.

Royal Fae Guardians

A complete Young Adult Urban Fantasy series featuring fae, magic users, a sweet romance, along with snark and humor.

Shadow Veil Academy

A complete Upper Young Adult Urban Fantasy Academy series featuring shifters, elves, witches, and more.

Elite Supernatural Trackers

A complete New Adult Urban Fantasy series featuring witches, demons, a smart-mouthed female lead, alpha males, and a snarky fairy sidekick.

Raven Point Pack Series

A complete Upper Young Adult Paranormal Romance series

featuring wolves, witches, vengeance, and fated mates.

Blood of the Sea Series

A complete Young Adult Paranormal Romance series featuring vampires, open seas adventures, and the occasional pirate.

Standalone

Marked Paradox - A complete Young Adult Fantasy fae story about a realm divided and one fae to bring them back together.